Bolan cautiously opened each door in turn

There were signs of habitation, but no guards...and no Grozny. Had they somehow got wind of an attack and moved the target?

Reaching the last door, Bolan listened. He heard the sound of breathing. More than one man, though one of them was breathing more heavily. He stepped to the side before opening the door.

He was greeted with silence. Bolan paused, nerves on alert, but calm enough to play the waiting game.

"You may come in, whoever you are. But carefully. I warn you I am armed."

Bolan recognised the voice. Slowly, holding the uzi at a nonthreatening angle, he turned and stood in the doorway.

Two guards lay on the floor, unconscious. Seated on the bed, legs crossed, an AK-47 nestled on his lap, Vijas Grozny, Balkan warlord, took in the man facing him.

"So, we meet again," he said. "You know, I like your style, but I have no idea what you want. Just that you keep turning up where I am held prisoner. So, in case we don't get the chance again—what is your fascination with me, man in black?"

"I'm here to make sure you reach trial...and that justice is served."

MACK BOLAN ®
The Executioner

The Executioner

Don Pendleton's ®

NIGHT'S RECKONING

A GOLD EAGLE BOOK FROM

WORLDWIDE ®

TORONTO • NEW YORK • LONDON
AMSTERDAM • PARIS • SYDNEY • HAMBURG
STOCKHOLM • ATHENS • TOKYO • MILAN
MADRID • WARSAW • BUDAPEST • AUCKLAND

Recycling programs
for this product may
not exist in your area.

First edition March 2013

ISBN-13: 978-0-373-64412-4

Special thanks and acknowledgment to
Andy Boot for his contribution to this work.

NIGHT'S RECKONING

Printed in U.S.A.

The moral arc of the universe bends at the elbow of justice.
—Martin Luther King, Jr.
1929–1968

When the arms of the law are tied, and there are no other roads left to go down, I will be there to deliver the final blows of justice as only the Executioner can.
—Mack Bolan

THE
MACK BOLAN
LEGEND

Nothing less than a war could have fashioned the destiny of the man called Mack Bolan. Bolan earned the Executioner title in the jungle hell of Vietnam.

But this soldier also wore another name—Sergeant Mercy. He was so tagged because of the compassion he showed to wounded comrades-in-arms and Vietnamese civilians.

Mack Bolan's second tour of duty ended prematurely when he was given emergency leave to return home and bury his family, victims of the Mob. Then he declared a one-man war against the Mafia.

He confronted the Families head-on from coast to coast, and soon a hope of victory began to appear. But Bolan had broken society's every rule. That same society started gunning for this elusive warrior—to no avail.

So Bolan was offered amnesty to work within the system against terrorism. This time, as an employee of Uncle Sam, Bolan became Colonel John Phoenix. With a command center at Stony Man Farm in Virginia, he and his new allies—Able Team and Phoenix Force—waged relentless war on a new adversary: the KGB.

But when his one true love, April Rose, died at the hands of the Soviet terror machine, Bolan severed all ties with Establishment authority.

Now, after a lengthy lone-wolf struggle and much soul-searching, the Executioner has agreed to enter an "arm's-length" alliance with his government once more, reserving the right to pursue personal missions in his Everlasting War.

Prologue

The trucks came from the west. They rolled into a village nine miles from Srebrenica, where the battle had been raging for days. The villagers had not wanted to take sides. They were majority Bosniak, and had little time for the Serbs and Croats who wished to rend their lands. Let them kill each other and leave tilling of the land and surviving the hard winters to those who had lived in the region before they had come, and would be here after they had left.

For over three years—since June of '92—the war had raged around them. They were in the hills, hard to reach by road and in many ways left behind by progress. While Yugoslavia disintegrated and blew itself apart in a slow and bloody way, they carried on living as they always had. Electricity was new and was still a luxury. Running water was a stream for some. Their wagons were horse-drawn as much as they were petrol-driven. The land was how they lived, and they avoided the larger urban centers as much as possible—barter and sale being their only reasons for venturing there.

Tito's life and death had meant little to them. The Communist manifesto that most knew by heart—on pain of death—was a mumbled oath that usually ended with a shrug. They had been left alone, and they left anyone else alone. That was how it had always been.

Not anymore.

It had been possible to hear the wagons from a distance, the engines whining and complaining almost as much as their drivers as they took the steep and narrow tracks that passed for roads, skittering gravel and rock down on the scrub that littered the mountainsides, disturbing the leisure of goats and their herders.

By the time the trucks hit the central part of the village, most of the children were cowering around their mothers' skirts, curious eyes peering out less with fear than with the expectation of excitement to break the monotony. Their mothers had impassive faces, stoic but hoping that their monotony—and thus their safety—would be maintained. The men of the village had been gathered from the hills where they farmed and tended their sparse flocks, the last few stragglers timing their arrival with that of the leading vehicle.

As it pulled up in a cloud of dust, the men raised their few arms, a motley collection of aging shotguns, WWII relics, and some even from the first war. It was a warning, a show of defiance…it was a token. But it was pointless in the face of a convoy that had obviously left the city some little time before, and carried armed men who were soldiers.

There was a moment's silence while the village faced the first of the trucks. Its windshield was an impassive mask of dust and watersplash that rendered it opaque. To its rear, the other trucks pulled up in a line, their engines whining, grinding and then falling to silence. Their noise was replaced by a sound that was more disturbing: the wailing of women in pain and distress, and the occasional violent sound of suppression.

The Bosniak villagers stayed impassive, facing the line of trucks, even though the sounds caused ripples of fear to run through them. Even the inquisitive children were somehow not so curious.

The passenger door of the lead truck creaked as it slowly swung open, and the first sight they had of the man who would become a terrible legend among those who'd survive was of his combat-booted foot as it hit the dirt, raising a small cloud of dust.

The door swung closed, and they could see him fully for the first time. He was six foot four, broad and barrel-chested, with his sweat- and bloodstained shirt open, revealing the still-livid weal of a scar that ran from his left shoulder down across his chest, bisecting the nipple and ending just above the navel. His tightly curled hair and beard were black and greasy, and his black eyes glittered as he took in the villagers with a leisurely sweep of the head. He held an AK-47 knockoff, butt resting in the crook of his arm, barrel angled up to the sky.

Hawking, he spat a glob of phlegm onto the dry earth.

"Yes…this will do," he said softly, almost to himself. Then, louder, he directed at the group of villagers, "Which one of you is in charge here?"

A middle-aged man, scrawny but with the wiry toughness of hard years spent farming, stepped forward. He held a shotgun of indeterminate age, with too many repairs to be anything other than a rabbit gun. But still he held it down, in a show of deference.

"I speak for us," he said quietly.

"And what is your name, man?" the soldier inquired in equally soft tones.

"Bogoljub. I am leader, such as we have it. And I'll tell you this—we have kept out of this shit-crazy war. Life is hard enough on this land without crazy Serbs and Croats wanting to kill each other. You want to do that, that's fine. You choose to do that, we won't stop you. But we don't want anything to do with it. We just want to get on with our lives and be left alone. That's not too much to ask. So whatever you want, if we have it to spare then you can have it. If not, then we can't help. That simple. So just ask, take and go. We want no part of this, and we'll say the same to anyone else who comes here."

The soldier nodded sympathetically as he listened to this. When the scrawny man had finished, he said, "That's a nice speech, Bogoljub. Very pretty. Good sentiment. And fair enough, you don't want to be dragged into someone else's war. That's understandable."

He let the AK-47 drop until it was leveled at the man, then tapped a three-shot burst that stitched Bogoljub from chest to stomach. There was still a look of surprise on the man's face as he fell back to the ground, his chest cavity mangled by the impact of the bullets.

One of the children—a boy of eight—broke from his mother's grasp and, crying and yelling, tried to make the dead man on the ground respond. The other men stayed frozen, the women gathering their children to them.

"Now, you have a simple choice. You can go along with what I'm going to do here, help my men and not be stupid. Or you can die, like little Bogoljub there," the soldier said in a loud voice, intended to carry to the back of the small crowd, as he gestured with his AK-47. "You can be sure that you won't simply be killed. For fuck's sake, I could have done that as soon as I drove in here. No, you can be of use. The choice is yours. What is it going to be?"

The men looked at each other from the corners of their eyes. They knew what their only real option was. One by one they placed their weapons on the ground. They did not look at their womenfolk. The women, for their part, kept their eyes on the bearded stranger, and did not look at their men.

The soldier grinned. Broken spirits were the easiest to use.

"I knew you'd see sense," he said with a soft and sinister chuckle.

WITHIN TWO DAYS, the village was unrecognizable. The villagers lived in tents and shacks that had been constructed on the edges of the settlement, while the buildings had been taken over by the soldier and his men. Apart from one: this was the largest building, and it housed as many beds, pallets and mattresses as could be gathered. Two doctors who doubled as guards took duty in rotation, while the other soldiers under the bearded man's command secured the territory around, rested up and waited for their next plan of action. The women who had been contained within the trucks were in the building, awaiting their certain fate with trepidation, their spirit already broken.

The villagers knew what was to happen—what had already been happening—to the women who'd arrived with the soldier. But the village women sneered that they were not Bosniaks, and so had brought it on themselves, while the men kept silent and just thanked God that their own wives were not considered eligible.

Oil lamps burned into the night while the bearded man and his trusted lieutenants held council. They were a strange collection, as the Serb and his two trusted Serb aides were joined by a Bosniak and an Oriental.

"You have handled this well," the Oriental said over vodka and cigars—for the Serbs and the Bosniak, if not for himself. "If you can establish a camp here, then it will be the first in this sector. Such a camp would, of course, require financing, with perhaps a bonus for the ingenuity and courage of the man who established it."

The bearded man snorted. "Ingenuity? I wouldn't say no

to that. Courage? Where does it require courage to gather together a load of women and herd them up?"

"Courage is more than just facing down twenty men with submachine guns when you have a rusty knife and an old pistol," the Chinese man said slyly.

The bearded man sniffed. "You've heard that story, eh? Well, let me tell you, it was true. To a degree. I was lucky. The first man to try to fire jammed his bastard gun. Gave me a chance to shoot him and get his. That gave me more firepower. They still would have had me, though, if not for some stupid bastard among them forgetting he had a grenade in his belt. One shot, man, I tell you I couldn't have made that shot again if I'd known where to aim. Took half of them down and damn near took me down, too. Again, luck. Did this to me," he ruminated, fingering the scar on his chest, "but at least it didn't take my eyes or my face. I could see enough to take down those fuckers before they could take me. Lucky, that's what they should call me."

"No," another of the Serbs said, banging his vodka bottle down on the rough table, splattering it with spirit. "What they will say is that Vijas Grozny was one of our best leaders, a man who took every opportunity that fate handed him with open hands, grasping it to his bosom and exploiting it to the fullest."

Grozny—the bearded man—threw back his head and roared with laughter. "You hear that, Xiao?" he asked of the Chinese. "That, my friend, is what a college education will do for you. Even when you are rotting your gut with cheap vodka you can still be eloquent. You should hear Bilic on the subject of this so-called 'ethnic cleansing' that we are accused of."

"There is no such thing," the Chinese said with a tight smile. "The United Nations cannot prove their contentions."

Grozny shook his head. "This is me you're talking to. It's

what I do. And why not? For generations the people in this land have been forced together to mix in a way that none of them have wanted. All sides want this so-called cleansing. They only pick on us because we have the greater numbers, and because what we do is more obvious. They're all at it, in one way or another. The Muslim and the Christian hate each other. The Serb and the Croat hate each other. Everyone hates the Bosniaks, right, my friend?" he added, clapping his Bosniak lieutenant on the back. "Truth is, no one gives a fuck about anyone else when they all live in their own little pieces of the land. All any of us are doing is trying to get everyone back where they belong."

Grozny sat back, looking dazed and exhausted by his rant.

Xiao smiled and took another sip of the tea that he had been drinking while the others got progressively more drunk. He was content to let Grozny rage in this manner. The more he built up his anger, the more he was easy to manipulate. The warlord was building a name for himself, and there were many in the Balkans who knew him by reputation. Karadzic was the big noise in this part of the world, and the Serbs listened to him. He got that way by being bigger and badder than the rest.

But Karadzic would not be around forever: already he was on a UN hit list, and if they could, they would let their peacekeeping forces keep that peace by illicit means. That was war. Equally, Xiao's masters had their own worries. Tiananmen had been a black spot on international relations at a time when China was beginning to emerge from the shadows of Mao. That was six years back, and things had not improved. However, the fall of Soviet-style communism, and its ripple effects, could do much to deflect attention from the East. It focused the attention of the West on the atrocities they could create themselves, and it created a fear of what may form in the vacuum left by the collapse of communism.

Some sections of the leadership in Beijing could see opportunities for stemming the regrowth of regimes that had not seen eye to eye with them, whilst at the same time forming a buffer between themselves and the West that was a little more oblique. Much of the Serb rhetoric in this conflict had been of the extreme right, not the left, so backing this would not be expected of the East.

Xiao had selected Grozny for the man's savagery, drive and his devotion to his cause. Also for his interesting mix of stupid and smart: he had the brains to lead, yet could not see when he was being guided by an ulterior motive. Perhaps in his zeal he simply did not want to see.

No matter. He would serve Xiao's purpose.

Two days after this, the work began. It was a work of atrocity that was yet enjoyable to many of the men taking part.

It was simple. Ethnic cleansing was not just about exterminating the opposition. Grozny and his men were good at this, and it was simple enough.

But once the Bosniaks had been wiped out, who would replace them? There would need to be more Serbs. More than there were presently—more being born to fill that gap.

And what of racial mixes? Over hundreds of years, hundreds of generations, this had been inevitable. Grozny believed that something had to be done to remedy this, and when time was tight then it would have to be an enforced solution. To balance the genetics was a simple matter of getting more Serb genetics into the mixes that existed, starting them on the road that would, over a matter of a few generations, see that balance restored to how it should be.

Impregnate the women. The Nazis had the right idea—they had encouraged procreation among the right genetic groups, even to the point of organizing homes where strong Aryan men could meet and impregnate strong Aryan women to create that required purity.

This, however, was a battlefield. In peacetime, there could be the right environment created. In war, you had to improvise.

Grozny was not the only one to do this, but he was certainly one of the most enthusiastic proponents of the ideal. He would refer to them in private as breeding grounds, but they would later be known as rape camps.

Grozny's men were of good Serbian stock. The women they had captured along the way and brought with them were not Serbs, but were Croats or Bosniaks of a mixed background—admittedly selected on the less than scientific basis of looking a bit Serb—whose descendants could have their genetic mixes restored to order, starting in the here and present.

Xiao looked upon this barbaric practice with an attitude that was both amused and bemused. It was a hit-and-miss, less-than-scientific method. But then again, he knew that in his country they took donated blood and mixed it all together, diluting with saline to make it stretch further: he was hardly in a position to sneer.

If his superiors had backed the wrong candidate, then Grozny would stand trial. If they backed the right one, then who would ever know? History, after all, is nothing more than the winner's story.

Nonetheless, as Xiao stood outside the block that had been selected, watching Grozny's men use their time off duty to go and impregnate the unwilling and shackled women within, he could not help but feel distaste. He did not relish any association with this attaching itself to him.

The native Bosniaks tended to the occupying force and turned blind ears and eyes to what went on in the village that was no longer theirs, thankful that they were still alive and were not under torture. Fellow feeling plays second to survival at such times.

Ignoring the screams and cries of pain, shame and pleading that came from the block, Xiao ground his cigarette under his heel and walked away.

FOR MORE THAN two months it continued. By day some of the men would devote themselves to the task at hand, while others were detailed to patrol the region around the village. Grozny had chosen it well—it was isolated and high in the mountainous hillside, which made it easy to survey the land around and also difficult for any forces to consider attack. To relieve the boredom of his men he would occasionally send details back toward Srebrenica, where the battle still raged on. The object was to obtain supplies, as the village was hard pressed to sustain its natives, let alone the new tenants. But in truth, it was so that the men would have an excuse to fight, to keep themselves sharp and to feel that they were still in the game.

Grozny—with a little prompting from Xiao—was smart enough to know that his men were easily bored. Unlimited and easy sex should have been enough to keep them in place, but the warlord and his doctors imposed a little more order on it than the men would have wished, and in truth it had become more of a chore than a pleasure to them. No one thought about the women, of course: they were there for the sole purpose of cleansing genetics.

The Chinese had another motive—the more Grozny's men swept in from the hills, made lightning raids and then withdrew before they could be followed or put to the sword, the more they would build a reputation for themselves and for their chief. In the long run, the boosting of Grozny's profile would increase his chances of success.

To look at it in this way prevented Xiao from having to think too closely—and thus feeling nauseous—about the day-to-day activity in which he had become involved.

He preferred it this way. However, it was not destined to stay at arm's length for long.

"COME, TODAY WE see if our little experiments have been having any effect," Grozny said over his morning coffee, slapping the Chinese man on the shoulder. When Xiao looked blankly at him, Grozny grinned. "It's that time of the month—or not…"

Suppressing the distaste and bile that rose simultaneously in his throat, the Chinese man left his tea untouched and followed Grozny across to the building housing the women.

It was the first time he had been inside, and the first thing that hit him was the stench. The women had been confined in too small a space for too long, and despite the best efforts of the two medics to keep some kind of hygiene, the disinfectant and bland odor of medication did nothing to mask the sweat and ordure that had inevitably gathered. Blood, too, though Xiao preferred not to ponder on the ways in which it may have been spilled.

Grozny appeared not to notice. His black eyes sparkling, cigar clamped between stained teeth and his black curls and beard glistening, he asked the medics in a hearty manner what results they had so far achieved.

Xiao noticed that even as they were led up and down the "ward"—for want of a better name—Grozny was focused on the medics and not on the women who lay blank eyed and moaning on the beds and mattresses. Come to that, even the medics preferred to keep their eyes on the warlord as they spoke, or on the charts that they consulted.

"All the women have now passed at least one menstrual

cycle since arrival, so we know that none of them had been impregnated before capture and arrival," one of the medics intoned.

The other added, "This is good, as it means that we can be sure that any pregnancy now is the result of our program—"

"I understand this," Grozny snapped impatiently. "You think I do not understand the human reproductive system?"

"I—I'm sorry," the medic replied nervously. "I say this merely to point out that any missed menses from this point on can be attributed to our men, and so we can begin to measure the success of the program from a baseline of zero."

"Very well, I accept your apology," Grozny said with magnanimity. "So what is the measure of our success so far?"

The first medic, who had been assiduously scanning his paperwork, spoke again. "Of forty-eight women we shipped in here, three died from wounds and injuries acquired during or before transit. Of the remaining forty-five, so far only eighteen have missed a period, with only two of those at the stage where we can safely say they have missed two. So we have a less than forty percent rate of success at present."

"What is wrong with my men? Their little swimmers don't swim? They can't get it up?"

There was a moment's silence, both medics exchanging glances as they considered how best to answer this without angering their warlord. Finally, the first medic, shuffling his papers as he spoke, said, "Our men have taken to their task with no little abandon. As for their own ability to father the next generation, I can only say that we have not had the opportunity to examine them in the kind of detail that we have the women. Certainly, for them we can vouch that there is no obvious reason why any of them should not conceive."

"Yet they don't…" Grozny looked around, as if seeing the women for the first time; which, in one sense, he was. "I suppose the conditions do not help," he mused softly. "But this is war, and we have no option but to make the best of our circumstances. We must continue, redouble the efforts. I suppose we cannot tell which man has fathered those so far pregnant?"

"We—er—have found it hard to keep records at times," the second medic stammered hesitantly.

Grozny nodded sagely. "Of course… A pity, as it would have helped. No matter. Time is something we don't have. Carry on."

Grozny turned on his heel and marched out of the building, Xiao was only too glad to follow at his heels. He was saying something, but the Chinese man was not listening. He took one look back at the interior of the building as he wavered on the threshold.

He had seen some terrible things during his service with the bureau. He would probably see more. But there was something obscene about this that went beyond war. He had an awful feeling that it would haunt his nightmares for however long he may live.

SREBRENICA WAS FALLING apart at the seams, the city decimated by the fighting that continued. But as this happened, so word of the prowess of Vijas Grozny and his men began to spread. They were fearless fighters who came into the city, took no prisoners and were ruthless to the point of cruelty. Torture to get what they wanted was commonplace. They needed supplies, ran the legend, because of the camp they had in the hills and what they were trying to do there.

It made him a hero to some, but a target to others. And

as the war ground to an inexorable close, and the United Nations Peacekeeping Forces began to make headway, so it became inevitable that Grozny would become a target. For everyone had their own reasons for wanting to claim him as their prize.

When the end came, it was swift. The Croats had come for him first, tackling the hills and finding that the entrenched positions of his men gave them the greater advantage. They were slaughtered on the mountainside. But they were not the last to come.

The United Nations came next, and they had the advantage of being fresher to the conflict. They also had tacticians who had worked out routes that stretched the manpower Grozny had at his disposal to the limit. They also had planes that strafed the village. But not bombed—the intelligence reports of women prisoners and villagers who were hostages, and the eyes of the world, put paid to this even though it would have been the preferred plan of those on the ground. Grozny was one of many warlords who would either be captured and stand costly trial, or else would be put to death in battle as an example—a cheap example, at that.

His men fought hard and bravely on their terms, but those who lived through the initial onslaught were driven farther and farther back toward the village. There was only a mile between the oncoming forces and the rearguard action surrounding the village when Grozny decided that he must pull the plug.

The sound of battle was distant but encroaching on Xiao's thoughts as he watched the warlord marshal his men in the village. The villagers, who had of their own accord returned to their old homes, unable to break through the ring of firefighting made by the clashing forces, waited nervously. Grozny's men in the village gathered what arms and supplies they had, dividing them up into packs that they could carry. Striding through the confusion as though he still had full command of the situation, the warlord waved an arm and at his command the trucks were set ablaze. It sent a clear signal to his men—and perhaps to those opposing them—that this was to be a scorched-earth policy.

Xiao knew that this was inevitable, given what he knew of the man, yet he still felt the bile rise in his throat at what was to come.

The villagers, cowed and subdued by six months of Grozny's rule, huddled in the center of the village. Grozny took two men, each carrying a BXP-10, MAC-10 knockoff SMG and led them over to the villagers.

"You said we would go free," one of the women said in an accusatory tone.

"You didn't seriously believe me," Grozny answered simply, taking an SMG off one of his men and tapping a continuous burst that raked the crowd even as they tried in vain to scatter. No one can be quicker than a bullet, and as the man who still held his BXP opened fire on the scattering villagers, it was inevitable that it took a matter of seconds to mow them down.

"Come with me," Grozny snapped at his men and Xiao, turning away without a second glance at the corpses on the ground. He strode toward the block where the women were housed, gathering two more men to him as he went.

Xiao felt that familiar taste in his mouth again, but swallowed—this was not the time.

"You, you, out now," Grozny yelled at his medics.

"But the work—"

"Is over. We failed, okay? Never enough time in war, and I should know that by now," he said bitterly.

The medics needed no second bidding and were already out of the block by the time the women—some of them presently heavily pregnant—realized what was to happen. They started to move, to yell, some screamed hysterically—but it was too little and too late.

Grozny opened the firing, his men joining in, spraying the room with SMG fire. The women did not have the chance to move far, and were easy targets. In the sudden silence within the block as firing ceased, there were no screams or whimpers: only the smell of cordite, blood and ordure, with the distant sound of battle getting closer by the second.

"We have fuel from the trucks, yes? Then torch this place. Nothing must be left," the warlord ordered.

He strode away from the block, Xiao at his heels, to where two of his men were waiting with prepared packs similar to the ones they already carried. Xiao looked back to see the first flames flicker in the block in an attempt to obliterate the obscenity within.

"Fuck it, man—that was the third time I've had to do that," Grozny said in an almost offhand manner. "If I'd had the time…"

Xiao watched him take the pack and load it on his back before taking the one that was offered to him.

"Every man for himself," Grozny said, raising a rueful grin. "Maybe I'll see you again sometime."

He turned and started for the hills without looking back. Xiao watched him, for a moment not thinking about his own escape.

The plan would no longer work. The warlord would be a criminal rather than a heroic leader. That was war.

Xiao hoped he would never have to see Vijas Grozny again.

1

"You have seen this?"

The newspaper was Dutch, and the middle-aged diplomat's grasp of the language was shaky. He spoke seven languages fluently, and had a smattering of eight others, mostly acquired in service of his country over a twenty-year period. He was presently in his late forties, with his receding hair cropped short and flecked with gray. He needed spectacles to read the small print. He was also surprised that the junior ambassador had brought the paper to him himself, rather than send a lackey. Come to that, he was not aware that the local press was particularly allowed on any premises belonging to the People's Republic. He spoke as he fumbled with his spectacles.

"My Dutch is not strong, but if you would tell me what I am supposed to be looking for, then—"

He was cut short not by any of the words that still swam blurrily on the page before him, but rather by the photograph that took up one-eighth of the broadsheet space. It was not a good study, being snatched as the subject was hustled out of a secure unit on his way to court. But it was recognizable as him, even after the best part of two decades.

The hair had grown long, the curls straightened by the weight of the gray-and-white curtain it formed. The beard was bushy rather than curled, where it had grown over the years. But the eyes…even in a blurred newspaper photograph they glittered and burned darkly. The lean face—more lined, and perhaps even leaner than it had been back then—was set as hard as the one he had known so well.

"Vijas Grozny. He has changed. We all have. But it is him. Unmistakable."

The junior ambassador curtly nodded assent.

"Then you realize why you are here."

"HE DOESN'T LOOK like some kind of warlord, does he?"

Simeon Boer was a young man, not long qualified, and this was to be his first assist in a major trial. He wasn't supposed to enter the secure area and look at the accused the evening before the trial was to begin, but it would never be his debut again. That was how he reasoned it to himself, and how he had persuaded Ronald Koemans to allow him access to the secure zone.

"What do warlords look like?" Koemans questioned. He was only a year or two senior to Boer but had been a guard for five years. He had seen a lot of warlords, and knew that they looked like the middle-aged guy who served him pizza every evening when his shift ended: like anyone.

"I don't know," Boer murmured. "I guess I expected something a bit more…a bit more military, or even bad-ass, I guess."

Koemans's mouth quirked. "They were badass and military nearly twenty years ago. But that's a long time ago."

"I guess. It's just that he looks like Santa Claus gone to the dark side." Boer shrugged.

Koemans snorted. "Then that is one Bad-Mutha Santa, that's all I can say."

Boer was silent for a while, studying his man. Finally, all he could say was, "Yeah, I guess so…"

While they had been talking, Grozny had been sitting at his desk, reading and making notes—presumably for his defense counsel on the morrow—but presently he looked up and stared straight into the lens of the CCTV camera. Even from the monitor, his eyes seemed to bore into the two men as they stood in the monitor room, watching him as he seemed to watch them.

Boer turned away, while Koemans, unnerved in a way that was unusual for him, switched off the monitor. It was poor practice, but he figured a few moments wouldn't hurt, and when he turned it on again, Grozny would have returned to his notes.

The two men stood in the CCTV suite of the Penitentiary Institution Haaglanden, about two miles from the Hague courthouse used for the International Criminal Tribunal for the former Yugoslavia. The facility housed its inmates in a relative luxury that had seen the building referred to with no little bitterness as the "Hague Hilton." Grozny had the same facilities as all inmates—granted so that the accused had the emphasis of innocent until proven guilty, as proscribed by the first judge of the tribunal. It was certainly a greater luxury than they would—or indeed had—granted those who had been under their governance. But then their own attitudes had changed: former bitter enemies who would have once taken great delight in the death of each other mixed and played backgammon and chess like old comrades within the confines of the prison.

Except, perhaps, for Grozny. He preferred to keep himself to himself, staying for the most part in his private cell. Like all the others in the facility, it had its own toilet and shower. With the satellite TV, radio and personal computer, he need barely move outside—except to make phone calls, as he had no private phone or internet access. He also used the gym and library, but shunned the rooms used for the varying religious denominations. He had no time for them.

He had long since lost faith in any God, and preferred to put his fate in his own hands. What he had been doing for fifteen long years before his capture was still a mystery, and his actions gave no clue. Any life he had made during that time had been expunged, and these days his life was solely himself and his defense counsel. He was self-contained to a point where it unnerved even the hardened men with whom he shared the facility.

He was focused, and the reason for this was about to become apparent, though not to Boer, who made his farewells and left the building, wrapped up in his own thoughts. As he left the compound, he did not notice the unmarked gray Ford truck parked in a side street. Nor did he notice the two cars—a Saab and a Volvo—that sat in adjacent streets, forming a crescent around the front of the building.

He did notice the distant sound of helicopters, approaching at speed. But he paid it little attention as thoughts of the following day filled his head.

Inside the building, seated in his cell, Grozny also heard the distant beating of the rotor blades, and spared himself the smallest of smiles.

"WHO IS THAT LOSER?" Milo asked, eyes following Boer as he crossed the street.

The man next to him in the Saab shrugged. "Does it matter?"

"Maybe," Milo murmured as he hit speed dial on his cell. It was answered on the second ring.

"Why are you breaking silence? And don't look over here," the harsh voice added. Milo tore his eyes away from the gray van. "Better," the voice intoned. "Make it quick."

"The guy just leaving…passed you a few seconds back…"

"What about him?"

"Familiar. Trouble?"

"If he was trouble I wouldn't have let him pass," the voice replied. "Name's Boer, junior prosecution grunt. Excited about his big day and wanted to see the Big Bad Wolf. Nothing for you to concern yourself over. You just stick to the plan, yes?"

"Okay…just wanted to make sure it went smoothly."

"No one likes a smart-ass, Milo. Just carry out orders. They're gaining."

The line went dead, and Milo looked up through the windshield at the skies. The two choppers were in view. They looked to be standard police vehicles, even down to the markings.

They weren't.

Milo could see that the man next to him was smirking. He shot him a look.

"Hey, don't take it out on me. You just stay frosty on what we're about to do now…" His Flemish was heavily accented, as was that of most of the men on this mission. The difference was that this man's accent was American, whereas the others were either from the old East Germany or were Serbs, and were accented accordingly. Milo had never warmed to him in training—a mercenary did not share your beliefs, and so was unlikely to fight with the same fire when it came to the crunch. Despite that, he was the one who had found the weak link, and who had plotted the battle plan.

As he spoke, the American took a Glock 23 semiautomatic pistol from the fast-draw armpit sling in which he kept it. He ejected, checked and rammed back in the thirteen-round magazine that fired 165 grain Speer Gold Dot

JHP slugs. There were other magazines attached to a belt that was slung across his shoulder under his lightweight windcheater, easily accessible for combat.

"Gentlemen, I suggest you do the same. It's time to go," he said quietly but firmly as he gunned the engine of the Saab.

The choppers were directly overhead, and as they started to move apart into a circular holding pattern that would take them around the PIH, they began to attract attention from the guards on the roof space, who could be seen gesturing and signaling as they used their comms.

Milo checked his H&K G3A4, another Uzi clone but less inclined to jam on continuous fire, and so was more reliable. His heart was pounding and his mouth was dry. He could feel his temple throb as the adrenaline raced through his system. This was what he signed up for, but now it had come he was terrified and exhilarated at the same time.

The Saab, Volvo and the gray van converged at the front of the PIH. The guards outside of the building were moving toward them, their own machine pistols held downward. Confused looks were writ large as they received panic and little information in their earpieces.

"They're still not sure," the American purred. "When the choppers start, then we hit hard. Our man inside will know to move."

Milo could almost feel the tension, smell the sweat and fear from the men seated behind him. For all of them, they had trained hard, but had seen little real action. Planting a few bombs and long-distance sniping were not anything like the up-close firefight they were about to start.

KOEMANS SWITCHED BACK to the CCTV monitor on Grozny's cell. Bad Santa, as he couldn't help thinking of him, was calmly closing his books, putting them to one side and then taking the furniture in the room and stacking it against the door. Normally, this would be a cue for Koemans—or whoever was on duty—to raise an alarm.

Not on this day—presently Koemans could only marvel at the calm of the man.

He switched to CCTV from the roof. He could see the choppers swoop over the roof, and hear the confused reports of the men stationed there. They were trying to raise the choppers, verify their identity.

Not a chance. He smiled to himself. They were asking him what was going on down there, and why he wasn't responding to their requests.

He finished unscrewing the access port to the comms circuitry, and traced a ribbon cable with his finger to its junction with a server box. He pulled at it savagely, tugging it loose. Three of the monitors died. He traced with his fingers to a group of wires welded into a plate. A bit more leverage, and they detached. The voices from the roof went dead instantly.

First part of what he had been paid for complete, he left the monitor room to undertake the next stage.

"WHY ISN'T THAT dipshit answering?" Heerdven yelled over the sound of the choppers as they swept across the roof, coming lower with each pass.

"I don't know, but then no one's answering us, especially those fuckers," his companion replied, unable to keep the tremor of fear from his voice as he scanned the air above them. Van Der Linden was an experienced guard, and knew that police choppers always responded—more important, they didn't make passes like this. Whoever it was up there, they weren't Koninklijke Marechausee, which is what their registration suggested. They could be high-handed at times, but they wouldn't act like this and not bother responding.

Van Der Linden raised his weapon, ready to fire a warning shot across the bow of the first chopper to pass. Heerdven looked at him, jaw dropped in amazement.

The older guard never got the chance to fire off a burst: his action precipitated the attack, as a rain of fire from the two passing choppers burst across the roof space, making guards scatter and dive for cover. Except for Van Der Linden—his action had made him the focal point of the first burst, and he was stitched across the middle of the torso, nearly cut in half by the heavy-duty 20 mm machine guns the choppers wielded.

Smoke grenades dropped onto the roof, laying down a covering fog that choked the guards and made it impossible for them to see what was going on.

Ropes fell from each chopper as they steadied and hovered, three men dropping from each, wearing gas masks and holding Spectre SMGs. The unique four-column magazines on each gun held fifty rounds of 9 mm Parabellum cartridges. It was unlikely that between them the men would be forced to reload more than once, possibly not even that. The Spectre would allow them to save precious time otherwise spent in reload.

The six men stalked across the roof space, sparingly firing at the guards as they attempted to return fire through the choking mist and tear-filled vision. It took only a short while to clear their threat. The six men knew where access to the interior lay, and made straight for it. The access was unguarded and unlocked, and in next to no time they were inside the building.

"Go," THE AMERICAN said simply as the first bursts of fire were heard from above. He was out of the Saab before the echo had died away. Milo followed, pulling a ski mask over his face. Most of the CCTV would be out, but caution was still essential. Behind him, he heard the doors as the two men in back of the car joined them.

Casting a quick glance over his shoulder, he saw the occupants of the Volvo also exit their vehicle. In front of them, the guards at the gates were calling warnings. They were obliged by their laws and by their codes of conduct to do this. Even as they did, they leveled their machine pistols in order to open fire.

They were not quite quick enough. Before they could squeeze off an opening volley they had been stitched by a hail of fire coming from eight men. It would have been wasteful under other circumstances, but necessary to get them out of the way so that the front of the PIH could be opened up. For while they had been clearing the way, the three men in the gray van had been calmly unloading from the rear doors two Hawk MM-1 semiautomatic grenade launchers. While one of the men—the owner of the harsh voice and mission commander—closed the doors and took up position with a short-range walkie-talkie headset and BXP-10, the other two walked calmly toward the front of the PHI and took up an anchoring stance before unleashing a barrage of HE at the front of the building.

The entrance was well armored, but even so it could only withstand so much. It was open enough to admit the men, and the blast had been sufficient to drive back any opposition on the other side, at least far enough for the invading force to gain egress.

"Gas masks. Lay down smoke. We've gained the roof and are inside up top," Milo heard in his earpiece. Like three of the men striding down the corridors of the PIH, he reached into the pouches that were slung under his windjammer and pulled out a smoke grenade, which he rolled along the floor. Lightweight gas masks were in the pockets of the windcheater, and were in place before the smoke had started to spread.

So far so good. They had made rapid progress, and apart from the guards on the exterior of the building, they had needed to fire only short bursts, and those to take out the CCTV cameras as they saw them. Most of them would be dead, if the inside man had been thorough—it would, however, do no harm to make sure, and would deflect suspicion.

Alarms were blaring, and the lights within the building had switched to red and were flashing. It was designed to make concentration difficult, but if the rest of the men felt as Milo did, then they were too focused to take any notice. There was only the objective.

The prisoners would be in lockdown. That was fine. All it did was keep them in one place, and made it easier to find their man. Not that he ever ventured far, if their intel was correct.

He would be waiting for them.

They made rapid and easy progress. The locks on all the interior doors were centrally controlled. The inside man had made sure that they had been disabled, and so they were able to move from section to section, level to level with ease. The blanket of smoke the team had laid down at each turn, along with the speed that the unlocking had given them, meant that the guards were taken by surprise and were unable to respond with the speed that they—and their masters—would have liked. Led by the American mercenary, the raiding party showed that their training had paid off—they ripped through the opposition as though they weren't there.

Speed was of the essence—the Koninklijke Mare-chausee would be on the scene as soon as they could mobilize. The PIH came under their remit, and although the regional force was competent, an attack like this was way beyond their competencies. They would have been alerted almost immediately to the choppers hovering overhead, and even with the inside man working for them, it was unlikely that no alarm had yet been raised, directly or indirectly.

As they reached the right level for their target, Milo found himself leveling his weapon at one of his own men: they had made it down from the roof with the same speed as his contingent had ascended. He grinned under his gas mask, wondered if the man facing him was doing the same and continued on his path, the other falling in behind him.

The PIH was a maze of wings and cell blocks, but they had rehearsed and walked through their route enough times to be able to do it even if there were no lights, and nothing but the blanket of smoke.

Then they were at their destination.

The American stopped outside Grozny's cell and gestured to his men. Milo and one other came forward and pushed at the door. It was secured by piled furniture. Why?

The pile yielded easily under their weight, and it struck Milo that it was too easy—the furniture had been placed for show. If CCTV was still working here, and if the evidence left behind was studied after, it would look as if Grozny had not been expectant or even willing. The old bastard was covering every angle he could think of, in case things went wrong.

They entered the room. Milo saw Grozny sitting on the floor in the far corner, impassive apart from the smoke-induced tears that streaked his face. Milo produced another gas mask from within his jacket, and as he bent toward Grozny he made to force it over his head. The old warlord raised his hands as if to ward him off, but slyly helped him to slip it on. As Milo and his compatriot grabbed the warlord under the arms, he seemed to resist, but once again

Milo could feel the power from his thighs as he thrust himself upward, his actions belying the impression he would leave.

Stumbling—this time for real as he was still finding it hard to see, despite the gas mask—Grozny allowed them to lead him out of the cell and down the corridor. He passed the communal rooms that he had barely used, and felt relief. At last he would be out and back in a world where he felt he had unfinished business.

Their part of the mission almost finished, the men from the choppers parted from the main group and ascended rapidly to the roof. As they went, one of them tore off his gas mask to reveal tumbling gray locks and a thick gray beard. He ripped off his Kevlar vest—worn by all of them—and handed it to a compatriot who stowed it under their own. In a plain white T-shirt, he could easily have been taken from a distance as Grozny.

As they exited onto the roof he started to mock struggle with his compatriots. Two of them appeared to overpower and bind his arms as they neared the ropes from the still-hovering choppers. Tying him to one line, a tug signaled for it to be winched up, the fake Grozny still appearing to struggle against the line as it ascended.

The other five scaled the rope from the second chopper as it was winched up and the craft joined its companion in abandoning its hovering pattern and circling to fly to the west.

As the pilot of each had expected, four choppers were heading toward them from the east. Each pilot had been nervously scanning the skies as the raid took place. They had one objective—to outrun the opposition.

But not without making sure that the fake Grozny could be seen by their pursuers as he was winched into the chopper from which he was still dangling....

FORMING A PHALANX around the warlord, the American mercenary led his men back through the maze of corridors, keeping point. They seemed to have wiped out all the guards on their way in, but you could never be too sure....

KOEMANS HAD BEEN keeping well out of the way. He had been well paid by the Hague official who had approached him. He had no idea who these people were, or why they should want to take the old warlord. He was well past his sell-by date, if you asked Koemans. But he had his own concerns—there were men holding a gambling tab that had been only too happy to receive the payment on his behalf.

The last thing he had expected was for these maniacs to come through here ripping a new hole in everything that crossed their path. The whole idea of making it easy for them to gain access was so that they would be quick and clean—that was what he had been told. Pity no one had thought to tell them, then. Koemans realized that if everyone else was dead or wounded, it was going to look pretty suspicious if he wasn't.

Koemans had the stupidest idea running through his head. He had to cover his own back somehow, and if everyone else had been shot at some point...

He made his way toward the entrance of the PIH. He knew that they would have to be headed this way, and he also knew that all the CCTV was out, so there would be no incriminating eye on him. All he had to do was to catch them and get their attention. Without, obviously, getting shot....

He could hear them as they made their way through the eerily quiet corridors, their footsteps echoing as they ran. He drew his own weapon and held it with the barrel up, resting loosely in his hand and in an obvious noncombat stance. If he was right, then he should be able to intersect with them just before they reached the exit.

THE RAIDING PARTY reached the front of the building, the exit in sight. Through the partially opened doors they could hear the distant sounds of sirens, and of choppers converging overhead. Time was of the essence. The last thing they wanted was any kind of distraction or obstruction: which was exactly what the uniformed guard presented as he stepped out in front of them, about fifty yards ahead.

"Hey, I'm your man, don't shoot," he yelled, his gun in a nonthreatening position. "I just need—"

"Out of the fucking way," the American yelled.

"You don't understand—it will look suspicious if I'm not—"

A short-tap burst of SMG fire cut him off. Milo let his hand drop as he saw the guard stumble back, stitched from throat to crotch.

"Good work," the American snapped as they passed the corpse.

Asshole, Milo thought. Both of them—it was stupid to make yourself known and stupid to call another death good work when the man was no threat.

That, he was sure, lay outside....

HE COULD FEEL the sweat dripping down his back and into his eyes. Fear prickled at him. There had been the sounds of combat from inside the PIH, but presently there was only a silence from within. With the coming of this it was easier to hear the approaching sirens and choppers of the Koninklijke Marechausee. It was coming from the east mainly, but he was damn sure that they would circle to cover all the avenues of approach.

In his mind he ran over the street map he had memorized. This was not a densely populated area, which was both blessing and curse. They wouldn't be snarled up by people and traffic at this point, but at the same time it would enable their enemies to gain quickly on them.

"Come on, for fuck's sake," he murmured as he leveled his SMG and kept an increasingly nervous eye on the streets surrounding him.

He was so tense that he still jumped when he heard them break out of the PIH and head for the vehicles. He turned and opened the rear doors of the van. Two men bundled Grozny into the back, one of them getting in with him while the other slammed the doors shut before jumping into the cab.

"Go, go, go," he yelled breathlessly as the driver joined him.

Hitting the ignition and grinding into gear, the driver said into his headset mic, "Plan Xero." Even as the words fell from his lips the Saab and the Volvo had squealed into turns that took them in directions a hundred and eighty degrees apart. His path was a ninety-degree split, down a narrow street that seemed to take them back toward the onrushing Koninklijke vehicles.

"Fuck, that's dumb," Milo breathed as he looked back over the seat of the Saab and saw the van turn and take its route.

"Never mind them. Keep your bastard mind on what you're doing—we're not out of here yet," the American snapped.

Milo turned back, biting hard on the retort that rose to his lips. The American was right. They had to get out of here in one piece, too.

But why send Grozny back, seemingly into the arms of his captors?

"WHAT THE FUCK are you doing?" yelled the man in the passenger seat as the van driver took a corner and seemed to head straight toward the oncoming sound of sirens.

"Trust me. We worked this out."

"We?"

"Me and the American. These bastards will be expecting us to head away from them, just like the cars and just like our aircraft. Fine. Let them think that. This way they won't be able to catch up with us so easily."

Although not a densely populated area, some of the streets in this district were old and narrow. It took some skill to guide the van down them and take the tight corners without crashing and either causing collateral damage or drawing attention to themselves. All the time the sirens grew louder.

"You're fucking crazy. Turn this around now," the passenger yelled, leveling his BXP-10.

"You're panicking," the driver said, keeping his voice level and never taking his eyes off the road ahead, although the sweat dripping off him spoke of the tension within. "Put that down, don't be an asshole, and just trust in me…now!"

With the tires burning on the road, he took another tight turn, bringing the van into a skid before reversing it up a side street. They were on the edge of the main road into the center of Den Haag.

"Keep low," the driver said, sinking into his seat. With some trepidation, his passenger joined him.

At the end of the road, a posse of police and military vehicles roared off the main highway and bore down toward the PIH. They passed the junction of the side street without pause.

As they retreated into the distance, the driver pulled

himself upright, chuckling as much with nervous relief as with amusement.

"Shit… I didn't think that would actually work."

2

He was waiting for them. How had he known where they were headed? Even as the blacksuit-clad figure stepped out of the shadows of a side street and into the roadway before them, Milo couldn't figure it out. Crazy bastard was committing suicide, he thought. Must be…

The Saab had parted company with the Volvo five minutes back. Over the roar of their engine and the vehicles that were in close pursuit, it was impossible to make out any other noises. Anything in Milo's earpiece was a garbled wash of white noise. There had been some indistinct shouting, and that was it. Radio silence was a good thing, but as they were closing in on the man who stood in front of them, Milo had the nastiest suspicion that the noises had been far from good.

The choppers overhead, that must be it—that could be the only way they had got in front of them. But even if that were so, how had this madman known where they were headed?

Even as this went through his head, he heard the American next to him curse loudly and try to throw the car into a skid and spin. But there was too little distance, and the street was just too narrow. Their route, in taking smaller back streets than the usually wide avenues of the city, had backfired at a crucial moment. The car bumped the side-walk and jolted, its perfect spin interrupted.

From the edge of his vision Milo could see the guy in the blacksuit standing—just standing. And then he raised a firearm. Milo didn't know what it was, but the American mercenary beside him, yelling as the car coughed and refused to yield, knew exactly what it was. An RPG7 rocket-propelled grenade launcher. The man in the black-suit, as calmly as though he was on a range, took aim and squeezed the trigger.

The front of the car was filled with smoke, fire and heat. Milo felt his bones crumple as he was thrust through a door that was mercifully already coming off its hinges. Merci-fully because this made it just that bit less painful to be blown through the gap: a pain that returned briefly as he jarred heavily against the cobbles of the street. He tried to scream with the pain—at least gasp—but even that was denied him as the air was driven out of his body as his ribs creaked and cracked in protest.

The very air in front of him was stained red. This was partly the concussion and the blood that streamed from the wounds on his scalp. But it was also because of the fire that came from the front of the car, turning the air around it red in the glow.

It seemed to him as though the man walked down the street toward the car in slow motion, slinging the RPG over his shoulder with a Desert Eagle .357 Magnum suddenly appearing in his grasp. Seeming to ignore the flames that licked around the Saab, the man in the blacksuit looked in the back of the car, and then in the front seat. He prodded the American mercenary with the muzzle of the Desert Eagle and grimaced in disgust.

He left the vehicle and walked toward Milo. Desperate, determined to go down fighting, Milo tried to grasp around him for any weapon that may have fallen nearby. It was a futile gesture, as he had no idea whether or not his gun had been separated from him in the impact. He also discovered that the impact had paralyzed him, at least temporarily, as his arms refused to move no matter how hard he tried.

The big man wearing the blacksuit stopped, standing almost directly over him, humiliating him in the fact of his proximity and Milo's inability to do anything about it. Milo could hear that the pursuit cars had stopped behind him, though he could not twist his head to see. He could hear footsteps on the cobbles behind him—three or four men. Despite the damage wreaked by this stranger, who was no way one of them, the Koninklijke men seemed unfazed by his presence.

"Grozny?" one of them asked. He then swore. The man in the blacksuit must have shaken his head.

"He wasn't in the other car," a heavily accented Dutch voice said. It was an accent Milo knew he could place, and this was confirmed when the voice continued. "They've been taken care of, no worries. And your intel was right. I recognize the driver. Been after him for some time, now—nothing worse than one of your own going rogue."

Milo felt like laughing, but all that emerged was an almost soundless gurgle of blood and bile in his throat. He felt like shouting that they had been triumphant. Grozny was still free, and the decoy had worked. He would remain that way. By this time the virals and the press material would be out there. People would know why.

It was a comforting thought. He would die very soon, he knew that—the red air was narrowing into a tunnel edged by black that closed in on him, and the voices became more and more distant, more and more indistinct. He would die, but the cause would live on, and would be triumphant.

As Milo left this world, a sense of satisfaction swelled to fill out what little life was left in him.

It was just a shame that he did not hear the rest of the conversation that was going on above him.

"MY PILOT TOOK out the other car from the air. I don't like showboating, but you left me with little choice."

"We couldn't move before we knew for certain. There were too many variables," the Koninklijke operations commander blustered.

"And there are too many men—your men, and good ones—dead because of that. I had to show our hand to stop further stupidity. But now I think I know what they've done—Kowalski was always kind of predictable like that. Everyone has an Achilles, and that was his. If you'll excuse me, I need to get this cleaned up before it gets further out of hand."

"You can't just leave with…this," the Koninklijke commander said, gesturing helplessly around him.

"Don't try and stop me," the man in the blacksuit replied with a hard edge to his voice. "This was supposed to be routine. It should have been," he added pointedly. Then, into his headset: "You get that, Jack?"

"Loud and clear, Sarge," he heard in his ear.

"Then what the hell are you doing still up there. Pick me up, on the double," he snapped.

"Sure thing. Just grab the dangly thing when it comes near…like now…" The pilot's voice was lost in the rhythmic thump of rotor blades as they settled overhead.

Despite the fact that his mood was dark, the soldier couldn't help but smile as Jack Grimaldi dropped the rope ladder right in front of his face with a nonchalant and almost impertinent ease. He grabbed it and started to climb.

"Get me out of here, Jack."

THE FORD VAN trundled into the flow of traffic headed toward Den Haag. In the cab, the driver and passenger had secreted all firearms out of sight. The passenger was still eyeing the traffic passing them on either side of the road with suspicion, though the driver could see from his posture that he had relaxed a little.

"There's nothing to worry about now, man. We are home free. All we've got to do is get that asshole in the back to the safe house, and we're sorted. You should have trust in the plan."

"It would have helped if I'd known the plan, asshole. If any of us had known the plan, come to that."

The driver shrugged. "I kind of figured that you did. I thought he would have told more than just me. But then again, I guess it's a need-to-know thing, really."

"Yeah, sure," the passenger said sourly. "It's just that you would have thought those of us in the vehicle would have known where it was going."

"Man, Milo was supposed to be with us. The Yank only switched at the last minute. I don't think he figured Milo was up to it."

"Right, so that's supposed to make me feel better, yeah?" He snorted. "We haven't even switched plates, for fuck's sake."

"No need. Wastes precious time. You see those cameras?" the driver queried, indicating the CCTV ahead of them and above the road. "Can't pick up plates, no matter what they say. Glare, shit and dirt on the metal. Better we get to the safe house. Turn the radio on."

The passenger frowned. "You want music? Now, that is just a little too laid-back."

The driver laughed. "Look at the time. The statements were released. I want to see if they're broadcasting them yet."

They sat in silence, moving lazily through the traffic, listening to the hourly news bulletin. The driver was careful not to break the speed limit or do anything else to draw attention to his vehicle. But as the news bulletin progressed, his knuckles became whiter on the wheel, and his jaw set heavy. When the bulletin drew to a close, the passenger leaned over and turned off the radio.

"Nothing," the driver said heavily.

"Perhaps it is too soon."

"How can it be too soon? We have Grozny, that is enough, surely? They do not have him. They do not have him. They must therefore know we are serious, and can back up our claims."

The passenger smiled wryly. "Maybe. But maybe it just means they've got a news blackout on because they think they can still catch up with us."

"Then we should make sure they can't," the driver intoned grimly.

"USING A .30 MM SMG TO take out a saloon car is a bit close to showboating, Jack," Bolan said with a ghost of a grin as he took the seat next to Grimaldi.

"Ah, c'mon, Sarge." Jack shrugged. "What else could I do? It's not like this baby is designed to do little jobs. The way they were crammed in there, our boy couldn't have fitted in. And if they'd carried on driving like that, Lord alone knows who else would have got hurt. Anyway, we shouldn't have had to deal with it at all. That's what those Koninklijke guys get paid for. You ask me, the guy in charge of the operation was a jerk who was out of his depth."

"Maybe," Bolan mused. "I get the feeling that he had pressure on him. Maybe someone wanted us to fail. Wanted Grozny to get out. Maybe even to get killed in the breakout."

"That's a lot of 'ifs,' Sarge. You really think it's that convoluted?"

Bolan snorted back a laugh and raised an eyebrow mockingly. "Hell, Jack, what do you think? Hal gets me in here and it ruffles a lot of feathers. Why do I need to get in here? What has this got to do with the homeland? There was a lot of crap that went down in the Balkans, but I'm not aware of anything that was either too much of an embarrassment or could be a threat now."

Grimaldi sniffed. "Kowalski didn't get involved for nothing. The only thing that made him ever tick was the cash, and a lot of it."

"Yeah, but who's throwing it around? I'm just here for some guy from two decades back who was in what was really just a local skirmish, looked at from our perspective. Why does he need to stand trial so bad? Why the hell does anyone want to go to this trouble to get hold of him? What makes him so important?"

"Jesus, Sarge, that is one hell of a lot of questions."

"I'd rather have answers, Jack."

He fell silent as the chopper cut through the skies. The police and military choppers that had taken flight after those that had carried the raiding party to the PIH were presently down, having failed to run those craft to ground. Dragonslayer was the only craft in the skies, and both men knew this would make them conspicuous to their prey.

"So where do you reckon they're headed, Sarge?" Grimaldi asked eventually.

"Back into the Hague," Bolan said softly. "I know what Kowalski was like. Bear sent me enough files so that I feel like I know the man. He was good. Greedy, but good— except that he had these little patterns of behavior, these little tricks that he liked to use again and again. You can get away with that if no one knows who you are or that you're on the case. But once they do, then you give yourself away. So he sends the decoy cars off in one direction, and ships the merchandise off in the opposite. Simple, works every time if no one knows you're the man behind it. But once they do…"

"Which is why we're going back this way," Grimaldi muttered with a tight grin.

"Exactly," Bolan answered. "Where better to hide a van and a man than in an area where such things wouldn't even be noticed? A blue-collar area where there are a lot of vans, and a lot of middle-aged guys who look like our friend Grozny."

"Which is why we're heading for the southeast of the city," Grimaldi affirmed. "Why this district?"

"Duindorp? It's on the coast. If they want to arrange a quick movement then they can use the port and not get caught up in roadblocks. It's run-down and there's a lot of empty property to hide in. And there's that local dialect. Hard to get the hang of, and my Dutch isn't too bad. Grozny could pass for a transient local at a push."

"The Haganezen and their plat Haags…" Grimaldi shook his head. "Had an interesting time in a bar round the dock a couple of nights back—"

"Interests of research, naturally," Bolan murmured.

Grimaldi shrugged. "Gotta know your territory, Sarge. Tight people, though. Stick together. Getting anything out of them will be hard."

"Well, that's not necessarily such a bad thing, Jack. You've got to love a sense of community, even though it might be a little misguided."

"Sarge, you sound like a man with a plan."

"No, Jack, I'm just a man with a phone." Bolan took out his smart phone and hit speed dial.

"Striker, I see you've been a little conspicuous today,"

Kurtzman's warm tones greeted him without preamble. "Good thing Hal isn't here right now, or else he'd have this headset off me before—"

"I think it may get a little worse before it can get better, Bear," Bolan cut across him. "Listen, you've been following this one, right? It's the gray van we're looking for, and it's got to be somewhere in the Duindorp district. That's classic Kowalski according to your files. Now the Koninklijke aren't too happy, either, but I don't think that's entirely down to me. Long story, but the point is that I can't ask for what I need right now without argument."

"Ah, Striker, you know I'm your number-one fan. Of course I've been following this. They've got a very good CCTV feed in Den Haag. I'd compliment them on their choice of system, though if I did that I'd then have to point out why their security is pretty awful. However, it has enabled me to more or less follow the route your boys took. Not always easy, as there are no real distinguishing features, and one gray van looks like another—"

"But you knew where to look, right, Bear? I'm betting you were way ahead of me."

"Neck and neck, probably. The CCTV is not so good when you get out by the water. Typical poor area, if I can stereotype. Either lack of maintenance or the local kids have good aim. But I've found it. Industrial estate, rundown and mostly empty. I'll send you a reference and also some footage so you can look it over."

"I owe you, as always." Bolan smiled.

"Teamwork, Striker. It's just that you get all the hard bits."

"That's the way I like it, my friend," Bolan said before breaking connection. Within moments, the map reference and footage were on his phone, and while Grimaldi brought

Dragonslayer round to head for the right grid, Bolan studied the footage.

The gray van entered the estate on a wide slip road. The units on all sides appeared to be deserted. Even the one that the van eventually entered had the appearance of desolation. He had to hand it to them: they'd camouflaged their location well. A deserted area is good for hiding, but it does make it all too easy to leave traces in plain view.

These guys had learned well from Kowalski.

"Jack, don't take me too far in," Bolan said. "Set me down about a mile out. I'm going to have to do the rest on foot."

"Problem, Sarge?" Grimaldi asked over his shoulder.

"You wouldn't be asking if you'd watched this," Bolan said ruefully. "It's wide open down there. They'd see you coming from a distance and be more than ready. Think I'd like to avoid that. And I don't know if you've noticed, but we seem to be the only thing in the skies."

Grimaldi chuckled. "A mile out it is, Sarge…"

GROZNY RUBBED HIS wrists and shook his head as he stepped out of the van, taking the step down to the concrete floor of the industrial unit and looking around him with approval.

"You did a good job. Perhaps too good when you had to make me seem restrained and unwilling, but otherwise good. Your masters will be pleased with you. By the way, would you happen to know who they are?" he added with a sardonic smile.

There were eight men in the unit: the van driver and his shotgun, the men who had accompanied Grozny in the back of the van and those who had been waiting in the unit for their return. A cell that had worked in perfect harmony and returned the target—returned him at great personal expense, as an equal number of their men had died. Those who had been in the van did not know this, but those who had stayed behind to monitor and coordinate had listened in to police transmissions. One of them, stocky, shaven-headed and eyes bulging with anger, stepped forward and grabbed Grozny by his T-shirt, bunching it up and pulling the older man to him.

Grozny could smell the garlic on his breath as he hissed, "We take down a whole fucking prison for you. We lose half our number to the scum that let these streets run riot. We do that because you are a hero, because you mean something. And all you can do is insult us. We are part of a group. We know who our leaders are, and we follow them because we want to."

"Are you finished?" Grozny asked gently. "Good," he added as a puzzled frown crossed the squat man's face. Then, before the frown could be followed by any kind of reaction, Grozny took the man's balled fist in his own, enveloping it with callused fingers that closed and tightened, causing the shorter man to gasp as his own knuckle joints were ground painfully together.

While his attention was thus distracted, Grozny brought his knee up sharply into the man's groin. The white heat of pain turned the gasp into a scream, his grip loosening. Grozny took advantage of this, letting go with one hand while using the flat edge of the other to chop across the other man's neck as he dipped in reaction to the pain, offering himself perfectly for the action.

He hit the concrete floor and Grozny casually rolled him away with one foot before looking around the unit at the men who were responsible for his release.

"One thing. Do not disrespect me. Remember who I am. I once took down twenty armed men. I was young. I could not do that again. Ten, perhaps. All of you, without a doubt. You know nothing. Your beliefs demand that you fight. That takes money. And that…that has to come from somewhere. We all have paymasters. Accept that. Somebody has paid you for me. They, too, have their reasons."

There was silence as he looked around the unit once more, then down at the squat man.

"Now that we have that settled," he continued in a milder tone, "someone get me a drink. And you—" he gestured at the squat man "—get up. It couldn't have hurt that much. No one has balls that big."

DEN HAAG IS AN old city, but unlike most of the Dutch towns and cities of a similar vintage—late-sixteenth to early-seventeenth century—it was not built within walls. There seems to have been no particular reason for this in any of the histories that Bolan had scanned while learning some geographic background. However, it did have the effect that while many of the country's towns and cities had suffered from the overcrowding caused by dense population and little movement for redevelopment that history had brought them, Den Haag had been given room to breathe.

The result of this was that the city had sprawled out in all directions, with redevelopments taking place on the fringes and causing it to grow until it was stopped on one side only by the water. There were rich and poor areas, like any city, but these spread farther apart as a result of the luxury that space gave them.

As Dragonslayer skirted the middle-class areas and flew over the deprived and rundown area of Duindorp, Grimaldi scanned the ground for somewhere he could either put down or drop the soldier. While he did this, Bolan packed a duffel bag and made sure the compartments on his blacksuit were put to good use. Some concussion and flash grenades, with a couple of CS and explosive thrown in; nose plugs and a mask in case he had to use the gas;

some C-4 and semtex with detonators and fuses, always a useful addition; a Micro-Uzi and the Desert Eagle that had once been his signature weapon, but found less favor as the nature of his missions dictated weapons that were more of an SMG nature; a Benelli M-3T with a folding stock and a switch to flip from pump action to auto. The latter was a gun he was hoping he could avoid using, as a shotgun in a confined space that included his target was always one hell of a risk.

But this was a time for risk. The Koninklijke would be following Dragonslayer closely, trying to pin him down. Nominally, they were the good guys like him—if only he could be so sure in this case. There was something rotten at the core of this whole operation. That was why Hal Brognola had asked him to step in. But Bolan was still groping in the dark, which made his mission that much harder.

No matter, that was for later. He was prepared only for the immediate objective—to secure his target. Anything else was irrelevant until that had been achieved.

Bolan made his way back to Grimaldi. "Okay, Jack?"

"Sure thing, Sarge. There's some open space around here, so I can almost set down, then get the hell out of Dodge. By the time they've realized that I've not just circled and carried on, you can be halfway there and I can be back—do you want me to hang around?"

Bolan shook his head. "Negative. It's a pretty static target. It'll be harder for them to track me on the ground if you're not close by overhead. Make them think a bit by heading off—maybe take your time, do some sightseeing."

The pilot grinned. "Gotcha. I'm on the end of the wire if you need me."

Bolan slapped Grimaldi on the shoulder and went back

to the hatch from which he would descend, waiting for the chopper pilot to position the craft.

Dragonslayer came in close across the tops of low buildings, a few curious passersby looking up at the sound. For the most part, no one seemed to care. The streets around this area were empty, even though it was early evening. The area was mostly light industry and warehousing facilities rather than residential, which helped. The fewer curious eyes, the better.

Grimaldi dropped the chopper down over a carpark that was almost empty, and Bolan let down the rope before sliding down to the tarmac. He seemed to have descended unobserved, and made immediately for the cover of a warehouse unit. He yelled a few words into his headset, and the chopper rose up, turning and veering off toward the east, away from his target location.

Bolan paused to take stock as he hit cover. Grimaldi's flight path would lead the Koninklijke away from where he was headed; and if by any chance the low-flying chopper had been observed by the target group, then they would assume it was flying blind and still searching. As far as the former were concerned, this was something he wanted to attend to with no interruption; for the latter, it was essential they have no advance warning of his approach.

As for Grimaldi, Bolan knew he had no worries about the flier being picked up. Grimaldi would give them a nice easy trail to follow until he decided to head back to whatever location he had picked for a base. Give them a trail, then drop under the radar, fly low and hard, and use the camouflage the veteran had no doubt already put in place until he was needed again.

Which would, hopefully, not be for some time. While this had been going through his head, Bolan had been checking the schematics of the area that Aaron "the Bear"

Kurtzman had downloaded. He had a route to the location of his target, and a clear vision of the territory around. All that remained was to recce the area on arrival.

He moved swiftly along the route he had chosen. It took him out of his way at times, but the blacksuit was conspicuous, so it was best to try to avoid being spotted. This did, however, have the advantage of bringing him out at the rear of the unit where the gray van had terminated its journey. He intended to make that termination in every sense of the word.

The unit was in the center of an estate that seemed to be in disrepair and little used. There were a few CCTV cameras mounted along the roadways, and from the footage sent to him he knew which of these were still working and should therefore be avoided. The cameras on the deserted units, however, could be a problem—likely that they were also inoperative, but there was a chance that the group snatching Grozny had wired them up to provide a panoramic recce of the estate.

Bolan had field glasses in the duffel bag, and he used these to get a closer look at the target unit. The original cameras on this were obviously broken: too obviously. A wry smile crossed his face as he noted smaller cameras, wireless, that had been fitted cleverly in secluded spots. There would be no way to disable them without drawing attention to himself.

Okay, then—if he could not easily get in, he must bring them out to him….

He began to circle the industrial estate, keeping to lengthening shadows as dusk began to fall, pleased to note that much of the municipal lighting was defunct, and placing the explosive charges that would be key to his plan….

GROZNY TOOK A HIT of the vodka they offered him. He could see that the squat man he had humiliated was keeping a distance, but the others had accepted his rant and were seemingly keen to pander to his every desire. It had been a long time since he had tasted any spirit, and although he had no intention of celebrating his release by getting drunk, he was keen to feel that burn once more.

He drained the tumbler and placed it back on the deal table, where bottles and a glass sat next to newspapers and a digital radio. He wondered what the headlines on tomorrow's papers would say. Given the scale of the raid it would be hard for a clampdown, but he wondered if the authorities would deem it wise to have his escape known.

For a moment, a pang of self-pity swept over him. He was a burnt-out warlord from another age—who would consider him dangerous anymore? He had spent too long in hiding and away from the fray. In his absence, all he had hoped for in the new country he had been trying to forge had been swept away by a tide of liberalism that denied its heritage and made it fit uncomfortably with the rest of Europe. Others who shared his views were like these men—outcasts and outlaws.

Why would he be important enough to make headlines?

Perhaps for what he knew about the past—there was still that, if nothing else. And that was surely enough to count for something, if not in the public eye.

He poured himself another shot of vodka and took it straight. It was smoother than the moonshine he remembered from the old days, but it was effective enough. It was only after this reflection that he became aware that the van driver was talking to him.

"Say that again?" he snapped, cutting the man off in midflow. "From the beginning…"

"I was saying that they have not issued our bulletins and statements to the people. We have a purpose, and you are part of that. This whole action, what our brothers have died for, was all part of that. We seek a new state for the Serb people, where we can have autonomy from the mongrel nations and alliances with pigs that have dogged us since the revolution. Only then can we make a state that will show our comrades in other parts of the East how things can truly be. Only then will real alliances be formed."

"And your statement," Grozny said gently, interrupting, "it was couched in these terms?"

"It was more eloquent. I am not a man who can phrase these things as well as others," the driver answered. "But yes, in essence…"

Grozny sighed. "Then it is no wonder that they did not run your statements. Let me guess—I have been released from an oppressor's captivity so that I can once again speak freely and help lead my people into this promised land? And then it goes on and on in such a manner for several paragraphs?" Grozny snorted, and turned to face the group. "You think they are bothered about this? What we Serbs tried to build all those years ago is nothing to them. If my release was a gesture, then it was futile and will gain you nothing. But if you want it to be more than a gesture, then it can be," he added, seeing the confusion writ on their faces. "First, I want to know who is really behind this effort, and why. Then we can talk about more than talk—then we can take action. Yes?"

"Of course there is more than this, but—"

"But nothing," Grozny roared. "Enough of this. I did not agree to this when I was contacted just so I could end up in another prison—" he gestured around him with the tumbler "—waiting for the police or military to close in on us. Why haven't we moved on yet? Do you people learn nothing from experience?"

"Calm down, old man." The squat man sneered. "We have a plan, and we are just waiting to be contacted."

"Yes, and I'll be bound that your plan did not include losing half your manpower and maybe leaving a trail by these means," the aging warlord snapped emphatically. "War is adapting to circumstances and making them work for you. Not waiting to be told what to do. Too soft…"

Even as he spoke, the men facing him were distracted by two explosions, a fraction of a second apart, that rent the quiet of the evening beyond the unit.

"You see?" Grozny yelled triumphantly. "Now *this* is what I mean…."

3

As the first explosion rent the evening air, Bolan was back in position and waiting for signs of movement from the target unit.

Speed was of the essence. Any disturbance, even in such a run-down and seemingly deserted area, would alert the authorities—and he knew that the Koninklijke would be waiting for the first signs to appear.

Keeping clear of the cameras and placing charges at three opportune spots, Bolan had covered an arc that swept the front and sides of the unit. His recce had revealed to him that the rear of the unit, although not having the large entrance of the front, had a loading bay that would also allow vehicular access. The space was tighter, partly because the egress was smaller, but also because the structure of the loading bay constricted any possible movements.

This was perfect—his plan was to use the detonation of the charges as a signpost to those inside that they were being attacked from the front, and that there were forces closing in a pincer. Their only option—assuming that they reacted rather than stopped to think—would be to try to ferry Grozny out the back and thence to another safe house.

Let them try this—Bolan would be waiting.

The rear of the unit backed out onto a narrow service road and the rear entrances of another set of units, which, like the target, faced a large car park. The whole estate had been designed on these lines, as a series of squares linked by the ribbon of these service ways.

Bolan had made the roof of the unit opposite the target and presently nestled into the shelter of the flat roof, a narrow coping for drainage giving him all the cover he would need. The shotgun sat beside him, ready to switch if necessary; for the moment, though, the Micro-Uzi was a better choice, set to trigger short bursts.

He waited, counting off to himself the gap between the first and second burst, then between second and third. There was no sign of movement from within the unit, and no audible notice that the blasts had caused concern.

A crooked grin swept across his face. Were they calmly preparing for evac, or were they rushing around like a chicken that's met the ax but won't give up?

His question was answered when the rear of the unit came to sudden and unruly life. The exit from the loading bay crashed open, and two men ran out, clutching SMGs. They were jerky and panicked in their movements, scouting the area around the exit and the service road—but not doing a good job of it.

Their actions seemed in contrast to the organization and efficiency that had marked the removal of Grozny from detention just a few hours earlier. Either these were men who hadn't been considered as good enough for the mission, or the loss of Kowalski and the others had sent them spinning off the axle.

Equally, either way it was a good thing for Bolan. He sat tight while they completed their ramshackle attempts at recon. After a hurried run up and down the street that would not have satisfied him had Bolan been their commander, they signaled back through the loading bay and into the unit. There was some indistinct noise, and then he heard a van engine come to life.

Bolan settled himself on the rooftop, and moved the Benelli nearer to his grasp while sighting the Micro-Uzi before bringing both hands to the SMG.

The van edged out into the road, almost tentatively, while the two foot soldiers kept point. They had settled into static positions that made them easy targets—one tap took out the man on the left, his head reduced to mush; a swing and a second tap stitched the other from chest to head. A wider target area to compensate for the arc taken in moving position, but still the emphasis on the head as they may have been wearing Kevlar. From the way red spread across the second man's chest, it didn't look like it.

Two down. The van had at least two more people in front that he could see through the windshield. How many were in back he couldn't tell: Grozny must be among them, as neither of the targets presented resembled the warlord.

Bolan laid down the Uzi with one had while bringing up the Benelli with the other. A smooth adjustment to bring the shotgun into sighting, and he was ready. He aimed for the fender, grille and windshield. With enough speed and just a little luck he could disable van and crew with two quick shots. Moving aim fractionally between squeezes, riding the hammer into his shoulder as he fired, he placed the two rounds.

There were twenty-seven shots in each round, and each of those shots was a .33-calibre pellet. Double 0 buckshot can do a lot of damage, especially if the distance is close enough that the shot doesn't spread wide, and is concentrated within a small area. Bolan may have been above the van, but the roadway was narrow, and the diagonal line of fire was such that the pellets were still clustered in such a way as to effect maximum damage.

The windshield exploded inward, and even through the haze of powdered glass Bolan could see that his shooting had taken out the driver and the man riding shotgun, both of whom were thrown back before slumping forward. The tires on the front of the van had been punctured, and the grille area was peppered with shot. The engine stalled and died—maybe it was the shot, or maybe it had been stalled by the dying driver. Whatever the reason, the vehicle was immobilized and formed an impassable obstruction to the loading bay.

Bolan was already off the roof and halfway down the side of the building before the engine noise fully died away to allow the commotion within the unit to be heard. Panic—just what he wanted.

With no longer a need to heed the CCTV cameras, Bolan took the quickest route to the front of the unit. They would have to come out this way, and he needed to pin them down before they had a chance to make good an escape. He ran down the side of the building, sizing up the cover that was available around the front.

Nothing. The car park left an expanse that was wide open, with the nearest unit a long way off if he needed to get under cover quick.

In the interests of time and wrapping this up before he had any unexpected company, there was only one thing to do. As he made the front of the unit, he took an explosive grenade from his duffel bag, pulled and rolled it toward the entrance of the unit. There was no sign of this starting to move, so without worrying unduly about covering his back, he veered away to seek cover and an angle away from the blast that he knew would hit....

Now.

Bolan hit the tarmac of the car park and felt the wave of the blast roll over him. He kept his mouth open to try to equalize the pressure. Even so, there was a moment of silence followed by a dull roar as his hearing returned, ringing painfully. Ignoring this, he rolled and came to his feet with the Uzi leveled.

Dense smoke covered the front of the building. Alarms set off by the shock wave formed a screeching background chorus. No one rushed to greet him through the smoke.

Let's hope it stays that way, he thought grimly as he maneuvered the gas mask into position and took out a CS grenade. He pulled and lobbed it across the gap between himself and the unit. He waited until it detonated—almost silently in comparison, or was that just his ears?—and moved forward quickly, keeping low and poised to mop up any resistance that remained.

Under the circumstances, he wasn't too bothered at that moment whether or not Grozny had become a casualty of this action. It would be preferable if he was still alive, or at least in one piece. At the moment, though, it was more important to prevent him from remaining free—at any cost.

FROM THE MOMENT that Grozny had roared with relish at the first explosion, a long dormant fire for battle awakened within him, there had been pandemonium within the industrial unit. Half the men were new to any kind of combat experience, and were thrown into panic by the unexpected. This had an effect on the four men who had taken part in the raid to free Grozny: their own experiences had been severely limited. All of them had experience of violence in a criminal context, but had never had anyone set an explosion on them.

Thus it was that the four who remained calm did so only by the greatest of efforts, and the van driver was pushed to the limits of his patience by trying to marshal the forces that had become, by the fact of his being the most senior man left standing, his to command.

"Shut the fuck up!" he yelled repeatedly, and for too little effect.

It was Grozny who took the initiative. He seized a gun from one of the men surrounding him and fired a short burst into the floor. It worked—a stunned silence fell over them.

"Listen to him. Always listen to your commander."

They were good words, but said in the tone of a man who could not quite believe the amateurs he had been delivered into.

Thankful for the aging warlord's intervention, the van driver sent two of the men out the loading bay to recce the immediate area, while he ordered the squat man to ride shotgun for him. The remaining four men were to get in the back of the van with Grozny and act as guards.

"We're to concentrate solely on the one method of exit?" Grozny asked mildly.

"The explosions have been at the front. This is our only chance…now hurry, for fuck's sake," the van driver urged.

Grozny said nothing, but made certain that he kept hold of a gun as he allowed himself to be hurried into the rear of the gray van. There were no windows, and it struck him that one well-aimed blast from a mortar could turn it into a serviceable oven.

As the doors were slammed shut on him, and on the other gunmen, he heard the squat man's voice shouting the all-clear. He sounded nervous, and inspired no confidence.

This was only confirmed when the van juddered to a halt that threw the men in back across the interior, banging painfully off the walls and across the floor of the vehicle. It stalled after two bursts of fire that echoed within the back of the van. Before that, Grozny had heard the chatter of

SMG fire, but no return. It didn't take much to guess that it was not the men sent to recce who were firing.

The five men spilled out the back of the van and back into the body of the building, Grozny careful to stay at the rear and slightly apart. His instincts told him that although they had been carefully drawn to the rear, that didn't mean that it was the only point of attack.

His suspicions were confirmed when the front of the building was rocked by an explosion that threw the four men backward. Remaining close to the rear of the unit, he kept a weather eye on the loading bay. Anyone who wanted to get in that way would have found it hard to pass the obstruction of the van, but even so, it occurred to him that this was not the work of a large force. Although the dust from the explosion was choking, he still felt that to remain here and see how the situation played out would be the best course of action.

Something that was confirmed when the CS grenade exploded with a dull *thwump,* and the cloud of gas started to expand within the small space of the building's interior.

It stung his eyes, scoured his nose and throat. Tears streamed from eyes that were already blurred by smoke and gas. But still he knew that he must take action—not against those attacking, as he was pretty sure that they would want him alive. No. While he still had time, he must make sure that he looked to be as much of an innocent and unwilling party as possible. Given the deliberate impression made at the PIH, this shouldn't prove beyond him.

Through the smoke and gas he could see that the four men had moved forward to greet whoever was oncoming. It was almost impossible from his position to see who that might be. But one thing he did know was that the way they moved left them wide open and easy to pick off.

So why not help? Making sure that he had taken cover,

he fired a short burst that hit one of them in the back, throwing him forward. This elicited a burst of fire from the car park beyond the smoking ruin of the entrance. A short, accurate burst, he noted, in that it took out another of the men.

Two left—both of whom had turned toward him, believing him to be an enemy intrusion. They fired indiscriminately, panicked shots flying wide of the mark. Nonetheless, Grozny did not wish to take chances, and returned the fire, taking out one more of the men. He was about to switch to the last man standing when another tap from the front of the building took out the threat.

Time to act innocent and dispose of his weapon: he threw it toward the rear of the unit, his lungs burning, and gave in to the fit of coughing that willpower and the need to shoot straight had barely kept at bay. Raising his hands, he yelled, "Don't shoot. It is Vijas Grozny. I am unarmed. I was taken against my will. Don't shoot."

"No need to say it twice, fella," a steel-hard voice returned. "Step forward, arms raised. Slow…" Then, when he did this, the voice continued. "Now down on the deck. Arms behind your back…"

Grozny did as he was bid, and felt handcuffs slipped on his wrists. He was then flipped over onto his back. Through the mist of gas and streaming eyes, he could see a man standing over him, a gas mask covering his lower face. The eyes bore into him.

There was a silence around them that puzzled him. He looked around, and even with his reduced vision, he could see that they were alone, although he could hear sirens in the distance.

"Just the one of you?" he asked, his voice a mix of admiration and surprise.

"JESUS H. CHRIST, STRIKER, I said this needed to be discreet and under the wire! What part of that did you take to mean that you and flyboy should turn into Rambo and a Thundercat?"

"Airwolf, Hal," Bolan said calmly.

"What?" Brognola's anger was temporarily waylaid by puzzlement.

"Airwolf was the helicopter thing. *Thundercats* was a kids' cartoon."

"Right... Nice to know that you have time to keep up with popular culture in between trashing half of the Dutch capital," Brognola snapped in icy tones.

"Everyone has downtime, Hal, even me. Now, you going to stop letting your blood pressure go through the roof and listen to me?"

"Give me one good reason why I should," the big Fed barked.

"You called me. Must be because you want me to report," Bolan said in level tones. "Now, are you going to let me?"

There was a pause—presumably Brognola marshaling his anger and reining it in—before the answer came. "Okay, Striker. Fair point. And it's not like you do that kind of thing without a good reason."

"Damn right I don't. The last thing I want is to have the locals all over me. I like covert. But this wasn't exactly what I was briefed on, Hal. I'm not blaming you for that, as you've never sold me short. But if you didn't do that to me, that's exactly what someone's been doing to you."

"In what way? All I have to go on is what my contact in the embassy tells me...and what I've seen on CNN," he added bitterly.

"Yeah, well, I'd be asking a few questions about your contact and where he's getting his intel. Then you wouldn't have to rely on TV for an update," Bolan said. "Let me call you back in five. I'm not as secure as I'd like here."

Bolan disconnected before Brognola had a chance to reply. He was on the third floor of a hospital. Down in the morgue were the men from the industrial unit. He still hadn't been able to get identification on any of them, hampered by the fact that he was back in his cover. All he knew of were the whispers that had reached him concerning their right-wing affiliations and a terror group known as the Serbian Unity Party. Here on the third, Grozny was in a heavily guarded side room. There was nothing wrong with the warlord apart from the need for observation and to clear out his lungs. In truth, he was here and surrounded by armed men purely because the Dutch were temporarily at a loose end as to where they could house him.

There were cameras everywhere on the floor, but as he exited onto the emergency stairs he noted that cameras were only on every second landing. A small but stupid economy but one he was thankful for as he found a blind spot and hit speed dial. This might take some time, and he had no desire for his presence to be noted in the meantime. He just had to hope that he could get a signal in the stairwell.

"Striker. This needs to be good." Brognola's tones were more conciliatory than the last time they'd spoken, but the concern was still evident.

"There is no good about it," Bolan said flatly. "I need you to level with me about this. When you handed me this one, you said it was because the Koninklijke and UN forces here were being compromised by leaks from within, and also because there was a possible source of embarrassment to the homeland if any action took place. You didn't tell me that one of your retired operatives had gone rogue."

"Okay, I knew Kowalski was involved. But this is not

about me wanting to cover my back against one of my boys coming back to haunt me. Kowalski has history with the Serbs. He's no spring chicken—"

"Was, Hal. I saw to that personally."

Brognola paused, then he said, "It was a different world back then. The curtain was only just down and that was one hell of a wasteland. We needed to make sure things fell the right way—"

"Did they?"

"Depends on your point of view. I guess you could say that they did for us in the end. There was heavy Chinese involvement at the time. It was a question of who would come out on top, and which of those warlords would be funded by whom. The usual."

"And Grozny was one of our boys, which is why Kowalski was involved?"

"No," Brognola replied, to Bolan's surprise. "Kowalski never met Grozny. He was funded by the other side. Kowalski was backing another nag for us—one that didn't have to go into hiding."

"Then why was he involved in today's snatch? Money?"

"I doubt it. Kowalski was an idealist. It was just that his ideals were not in tune with the administration's."

"So he was a true believer. But it would drag up too much dirt if he was discovered to be involved now?"

"Right. And you've got him nailed and right under your feet. Did you ID him?"

"None of them have been ID'd as far I know. Leave him to me, Hal. Was he the only reason I was here, or is there more?"

"Whispers. The Chinese have an interest."

"Why? It makes no sense."

"As I hear it, it's not part of an overall strategy, but things are changing in Beijing. There are factions within the regime that have a few skeletons rattling a little too loudly. Grozny being on trial could bring those out of the cupboard and into a little harsh daylight."

"Just rumors?"

"There's a new attaché flown into the embassy in the Hague. His name is Xiao Li, and intelligence puts him in the right place at the right time to have been the legman between that regime and Grozny. It might just be coincidence—"

"But that's not likely, is it? Do your whispers tell you if the Chinese have anyone inside the security systems surrounding the UN and the Hague, because there are holes everywhere you look. There's either too much complacency, or there are a lot of people with dual agendas."

"That bad, eh?"

"Do I ever exaggerate, Hal? My contact is good. I trust him and he keeps his ear close to the ground. It was thanks to him that I was able to get to the PIH today."

"I think you'd better fill me in on that, Striker. Just what did happen?"

Bolan briefly outlined the events that led him to the hospital. When he had finished, he added, "I asked Jack to hang around, just in case I needed him. I had no other backup, and within twenty-four of arriving I had a bad feeling about this. I got onto Bear and got him to rustle up Jack from whatever flyboy bar he was R & R-ing. I didn't want to be so conspicuous, but the way the authorities here were moving, it had fail written all over it."

"Deliberate?"

"Up the ladder…not the boys on the ground. They can only respond to what they're given, and I just felt they were being constrained."

"Cover blown?"

"As long as I don't see any of these Koninklijke guys,

then maybe I can keep it going a bit longer within the Hague. But I'm on the clock. It helps that it's chaos here, and no one's worrying about an IT consultant who didn't show for work today. I did remember to call in sick," Bolan added with a chuckle. Then, voice hardening, he said, "PIH is out of action for a while. There are repairs to the comms and surveillance systems, and some structural damage. They were thorough. The worst of it is that they cut down everyone who crossed their path. Which means that we can't even find the inside man—and there must have been one—and follow the chain. They made sure of that. Maybe that's why they killed any guard in sight."

"Word has it that they've got maximum-security spaces for all the inmates left behind."

"I'm so pleased," Bolan replied heavily. "What about our man? He has half a detachment around him right now, but if there's another cell out there waiting to make a move, I'd hate it if they had the chance to come down here."

"Not going to happen. Grozny is being moved to a safe house by the Hague, away from the other PIH inmates. A secured location."

"No such thing here, Hal. I'm going to have to shadow Grozny if he's going to reach trial without anything else going down. I'm assuming that even though Kowalski is dead, the Chinese connection could still drag up a lot of things—"

"—that the current administration wouldn't like to have to account for. Right."

"I'll deal with Kowalski first, then liaise with the contact," Bolan said.

"Keep it low-key, Striker."

"I'll try, Hal. Just don't watch CNN until the trial starts."

THE MORGUE WAS almost deserted. Only the duty porter remained, under a single light, feet on the table and a

Nintendo in his hand. Bolan was a little surprised that the bodies were not under guard to prevent tampering or snatching, but figured that manpower was stretched and it was unlikely that dead men were going anywhere.

One of them was. The morgue attendant was too engrossed in his game, and Bolan was able to sidle up and disable him with a single movement.

None of the drawers were name-tagged as there had been no ID, so the soldier had to swiftly go through them in order until he reached his man. Kowalski had been disfigured, but not so badly that Bolan did not recognize his face. Prints and dental would be too easy to trace. He could either obliterate them, which may take a little time in the case of dental work, or he could just take the body and dump it.

No. Better to get the body out and then dispose of it himself. He secured a gurney and transferred the corpse before heading for the exit. He removed the porter's uniform coat for disguise, and found progress was remarkably easy. Perhaps not. Who was concerned with a porter and a gurney going out rather than coming in, considering the situation three floors up?

Out the back of the building, it was easy at this time to find an ambulance that had just discharged its cargo. The paramedics were both in Emergency. It was the work of a moment to stow the body—there was no need for finesse—and then hot-wire the vehicle. He was out of hospital grounds before the crew even realized their vehicle was gone.

It was only when he was several blocks from the hospital that he took out his cell and hit speed dial.

"Hey, Sarge, didn't think I'd be hearing from you again today. See we made the lead on local TV?"

"Yeah, funny, Jack, real funny.... I'll get Hal to call you and tell you what he thinks of that. Are you busy?"

"Well—"

"Rhetorical question, Jack. I've got something I need you to help me dispose of safely. How long will it take you to get to me if I activate my GPS?"

4

The following morning saw a red-eyed IT expert named Matt Cooper back on duty at his post at the Permanent Court of International Justice, from where he was outsourced to the adjuncted courts representing war crimes and human rights abuses that seemingly multiplied by the day, each bringing its own problems when it came to IT security.

"Good to see you back, Matt," Belinda Hagen murmured as she walked by his desk. "Where were you yesterday? The new Syria unit? I hear they need setup, and quick."

Bolan rubbed his eyes then shook his head as he looked up from his monitor. Ostensibly, he was trying to find a back door in a new security system to test its validity. Truth was that Kurtzman had sent him the procedure for cracking it and then patching the night before, ready for his day's cover work, along with a lengthy diatribe about the slackness of UN security. Looking at how simple it would be, he could only agree, and wondered how he could make this look like a day's work while in pursuit of his own agenda.

Hagen was in her early thirties, a blond lawyer who was definitely career driven but had an air of loneliness about her. She'd been taking an interest in the dark stranger since he had arrived. Not that Bolan didn't like her, but this was not the place. He had already wasted too much time trying to deflect her actions without arousing any animosity—and it looked as if he had to do it again.

"I wish I had been over there yesterday, Bel. A clean new system is easier to work with than the bug-ridden crap they've landed you with here. But I was off sick. I hear it was all action round town while I had my head down the john after some seriously offensive seafood."

As a cover story, it was intended to explain absence, lack of contact and also put off anyone who wanted further detail. It didn't take the amorous into account, however.

"You poor thing…" Hagen took him by the chin, lifting his head and looking into his eyes, taking Bolan's lack of rest for sickness. "You have to be careful where you eat, even in a high-maintenance city like this. You should let me be your guide—"

"I'll bear that in mind, but I don't think I'll be wanting seafood for some time yet."

"Oh, I can be your guide for anything," she said in what she hoped was a seductive voice.

"I'll bear that in mind," Bolan said hurriedly. He wanted to get rid of her, but then his attention was taken by the pile of newsprint she was carrying, the top sheets of which were English rather than Dutch. "I've got some catching up to do…looks like you have, too?"

She sighed, placing the papers before him. "You picked a good day to be sick, if that can be said. All hell broke loose yesterday, and in the department for the former Yugoslavia, too. That's hardly a current situation."

"I heard whispers this morning, but there was nothing public I caught," Bolan said carefully.

"That's because our people tried to keep it under wraps, but how can you do that when some bunch of crazies try to blow up a prison building and our own military act like they're in the Middle East? It was like a war zone out there, and they thought they could keep it quiet."

"Seemed to work. Nothing I saw. Haven't heard too much since I've been in, either."

Hagen laughed. Her smile was momentarily distracting, although Bolan was concerned to know how much of his own anonymous involvement may have made the media. His cover was already on tenuous ground.

"Honey, you wouldn't believe it. First an air attack on the PIH with multiple fatalities, followed by what looks like a car chase out of Mi4. It all went a bit Hollywood, and ended up with some kind of shootout on an industrial park. I know our boys had to bring it to a swift end, but they could have been a bit more subtle."

"What was it about?" Bolan probed as he tried to rapidly scan the international papers without seeming too interested. The local press had been curt, and he hadn't had a chance to scan the Net as yet. But this didn't look good.

Hagen shook her head. "I don't get it, really. They took this guy Grozny, who's minor, as far as these old Balkan guys go. Our national intelligence sat on the material released to the press here, but couldn't stop it leaking out across the border."

Satisfied that the Koninklijke had been more than happy to take any credit going and so had inadvertently given himself and Grimaldi the screen they needed, Bolan had moved on down the pages to note that the cell effecting the breakout had been keen to release a triumphant press release about the restoration of Grozny to his rightful place at the head of a Serb revolutionary council.

Once the old man had been settled into his safe house before his trial, Bolan would be glad to ask him a few questions about this revolutionary council. If his own intel had been correct, the old man had been made a figurehead with minimal involvement on his part.

The big questions—why, and who?

He would have to seek some intel from his own source in the Hague—the only one he was sure he could trust.

"You know, they're going to have their hands full getting that house back in order over there. Looks like it took out their systems as well as their men. I have a nasty feeling they're going to be calling on me, which means I'm going to have to get this back door fixed before I leave you. I really must—"

He indicated his terminal, and handed the newsprint pile back to the blond lawyer. She looked at him a little crestfallen.

"Oh…well, don't forget my offer," she said weakly.

"I won't," he said, deliberately fixing his attention on the screen. "I might be a little busy, though…" He glanced up as she moved away, and not without a little regret, considering the way she moved across the room.

Somehow, though, he figured things were not about to let up enough for anything enjoyable.

"YOU ARE LATE," the Chinese man murmured mildly, yet with enough rebuke in his tone to make his companion wince.

"It was not my intent to cause you offense. You know that we value your continued support of our cause, and would not wish to imply any disrespect toward you or your government."

Xiao Li took off his spectacles and sighed as he polished them before placing them back on the bridge of his nose. He took in the heavyset man who stood before him.

"Your mealymouthed platitudes mean little to me. Or, it

must be said, to those I am answerable to. You did not do a good job yesterday. In truth, it was lamentable."

"That is a little unfair. We had factored in the military and the police forces that we would encounter. We dealt with their threat well enough and got our man away from them. We can hardly be blamed for what happened."

"And just what did happen?" Xiao asked in mild tones. "It would appear to all intents and purposes that you allowed one man, acting seemingly independent of the military, to not only neutralize your men but also recapture the target."

"There was no way we could factor in whoever the hell that was," the heavyset man returned heatedly. "We—"

"You do not know who he was?" Xiao interjected. "That is most illuminating. Perhaps we should be looking for better avenues—those who are more productive—in which to invest our time and capital."

"Capital—I like that. Your people have adapted well to the language of the West," the heavyset man sneered.

"Adaptability and the willingness to bend with the winds rather than snap are not values that should be overlooked. You would do well to learn that if you are to have a second chance," Xiao counseled. "Walk with me."

Slowly, and in silence, he began to pace around the room. The men were standing among tourists and students in the Panorama Mesdag building, housing a cyclorama of 15 yards in height and a diameter of about 47 yards, which made for a circumference of 120 yards. Painted by Hendrik Mesdag at the beginning of the 1880s, the cyclorama gave the viewer the impression that they were standing on dunes above sea level, looking down at the sea, the beach and the buildings of Scheveningen. There was a false bottom to the painting that landscaped into the floor of the building, enhancing the illusion. Xiao had wanted to see this place since arriving in Holland, and it served its purpose well. To all intent, it seemed as though he was just a minor diplomat on an afternoon off, taking in some local culture, who happened to be talking to one of several people he had exchanged pleasantries with on this trip. He had been careful to arrive before the allotted time and so establish this before his contact arrived.

It had another purpose, one that may not have been obvious to the man walking beside him.

"You must be aware that the way in which things appear to the world may not necessarily be the way they are," he said carefully. "Consider this room, for example. We know that we are not seeing an actual world before our eyes, only a representation of one. One, nonetheless, that is designed to make us believe that we are in another place."

The heavyset man looked at him blankly. "I don't…" he said slowly.

Xiao sighed. "You desire a leader. We have been more than happy to help you in procuring that leader. A man who, in the past, was an ally of ours, much as you are now. But now, as then, we acted because it best suited us, not necessarily because we would wish to be associated with the aims and ideals of that man or those he represented. In the same way, we would wish to stay in the background now."

"This I understand. I still don't see—"

"Of course, your plan to make your aims known to the world by way of your announcement was shortsighted. It took some assistance and some trouble for us to increase the spread of your manifesto beyond your stunted efforts. And I would wish you to consider the equally stunted efforts you may make in attempting to take once more your target."

"Are you saying that we should not make another attempt?"

Xiao stopped before a section of cyclorama that presented a calm seascape. "I am fond of this section. Changing yet unchanging. Like all of us.... No, I do not say that. What I wish you to consider is this. Your aims would assist us in changing the political landscape in a delicate area. Your erstwhile leadership figure is a man whose reputation we helped to forge. However, you would do well to consider that I knew him, and thus know of his own instinct for self-preservation. You should perhaps question why, of all the people in that building, he came out unscathed while all your men died. Interesting that he managed to avoid any kind of crossfire. Not, if you know your history, the first time this has happened to him.

"Consider this, if you will. An idol with feet of clay can bog down the path to a revolution. A martyr on a pedestal stands as a shining beacon to light the way."

The heavyset man pursed his lips and scrutinized Xiao carefully. "Are you saying what I think you are?"

A faint smile crossed Xiao's lips. "I make only remarks upon the nature of heroic figureheads. Their best purpose is up to you. And if that purpose is best, then it will have our full support. Now...is it not wonderful the way that sea appears to follow you around the room?"

The heavyset Serb assented, realizing that his audience had just been brought to a conclusion.

"You know the problem with this place? Unless there's a real, serious world conflagration, then no one is actually going to give a shit about who lives and who dies. You can have millions scattered across the globe dying every day in a battle of some kind, but unless it gets to really big numbers concentrated in one region, then it's not going to show up on the balance sheet and screw up someone's budget. It's only when that happens that we'll get some kind of action. Until then, it's guys like you who have to do the firefighting, and that's all it is, man. No one actually gives a crap about solutions."

"That's an interesting point of view," Bolan said mildly. "And I should imagine it would make you very unpopular if you voiced it too loudly in these parts," he added.

The young man facing him took a long pull on the Starbucks latte in front of him, and sucked in hard.

"Globalization my ass—it doesn't taste like it does back home." He shook his head sadly. "Sorry, Mr. Cooper, rant over. It just really pisses me off some days."

"Don't be," Bolan said quietly. "I agree with you. I've been fighting all my life and I'd like nothing better than to hang up the spurs. But it still goes on. Sure, part of it is just human nature and cussedness. But part of it is greed, and that's the same thing that you're talking about, only from a different perspective. Budgets, assets…everyone wants a slice of the pie. And while they're arguing about it, innocent people are dying."

Gordon Clelland sat back in his seat and nodded. "You know, sir, when I signed up for all this straight out of college I figured that with it being the Agency, there was a chance of really doing some good. Of course, it's the Homeland that's my number-one priority, but seeing as part of that is the Constitution and the idea of freedom, I can't see that as a problem. Soon found out I was wrong there."

"I guess that's why Hal scoped you out and got you onside."

"I'd like to think so. Mr. Brognola trusts me and I like to reciprocate. See, the idea of the Agency and what we're supposed to be doing here is fine and good, but it never works out that way. Too much territorial pissing and that leaves gaps where the bad guys can sneak in. I guess I like to think of myself as just watching those gaps. I get plenty of opportunity."

They were seated in a Starbucks a few blocks from the main Hague offices of the NC3A, the agency responsible for the procurement and development of C3 capabilities to a number of NATO bodies including Allied Command Transformations and Allied Command Operations, as well as a number of smaller divisions with the NATO model. With its emphasis on prototyping and spiral-growth models, it was about equipping the areas of NATO with the best systems in hardware, software and management to ensure the smooth running of the engine for global peacekeeping. Five hundred operatives worked in the Hague, with another three hundred based in Brussels. They came from many countries, and yet for the most part their true allegiances were departmental, with each determined to fight their own corner without looking at the whole.

The bureaucrat's disease, Clelland had called it the first time he had met with Bolan. From his position, he had seen it spread across all the agencies in the Hague, so that none fully collaborated with the others.

"I have to be honest, I was still in school and thought Nirvana was the most important thing to happen to me since Slayer, when the Balkans war was going down in the nineties," Clelland continued. "I know about it now, but only through secondhand reports. A bit like the assholes who blew the PIH apart. Why the Dutch government thought it could keep their manifesto down is beyond me. I'll tell you one thing, though. As far as I can tell, the Serbs only released it to the Dutch press, which is maybe why the government took the chance. Which means just one thing, right?"

"Someone else leaked it to the wider world. Perhaps

someone who has a hand in financing what would have been a pretty expensive operation for a small group."

"Exactly, Mr. Cooper. Now, Mr. Brognola tells me that there were always rumors of the Chinese being interested in the Balkans. If nothing else, it would be a nice distraction for the world away from Tiananmen, right? That would figure, especially as with Soviet communism dead in the water there was a lot up for grabs. Question is, what would they get out of it now?"

"China wants to be Westernized and create some kind of communist/capitalist hybrid. Why dig up the past that can embarrass that? I need hard evidence and facts, Gordon. I can't act unless I have something solid to work with."

"I understand that, Mr. Cooper. Really, I do. But we're working with shadows and light here. If Grozny goes to trial, then he can try to save his skin by dumping a few old friends in it—he could do that, anyway, just for the hell of it. He sounds like the kind of guy who would. So maybe it'd be good for them to help get him away from the public arena."

"But this Serb group wants an ethnic-cleansing regime that would create a new separatist state with Grozny at the head. Not exactly a way to keep him quiet."

"Maybe not, Mr. Cooper. But there's a new junior attaché at the Chinese embassy. Kind of old for a junior, but rumor has it he fell out of favor after a promising early career. Which, and again it's only rumor, has him in the Balkans around the turn of the nineties."

"A different kind of Slayer," Bolan mused.

Clelland laughed. "I like it. Thing is, I've been wondering what the Chinese get out of it, what the Serbs get out of it and what Grozny gets out of it, and I keep coming back to the same thing."

"Which is?"

Clelland drained his latte before speaking. "You don't have to be alive to be a figurehead. Everyone's a winner in that instance. Except Grozny, of course."

Bolan grimaced. "Which is exactly why someone has to keep the bastard alive...and get him to the courtroom."

DEN HAAG HAS A life that centers around Hofvijver and Binnenhof, the central areas of the old city where the Parliament and the main NATO and International Justice buildings are located. These areas, in the main, consist of old buildings with spaces cleared for the new bureaucratic offices. Housing, such as it is, is cramped and expensive. And, most important, difficult to defend and police effectively. For this reason, Bolan was sure that none of the safe houses in this area would be used for holding Grozny.

However, to the northwest of the city was an area called Belgisch Park. This was an affluent area, and as such was full of wide roads, tree-lined streets and open spaces, and large houses in their own small grounds, most of which had been constructed between 1870 and 1940. It was also pretty sparsely populated, a natural corollary of this kind of building, with less than eight thousand residents within the area.

And, with a sense of irony that appealed to Bolan, to the east of the area was Scheveningen, location of the recently decimated PIH. To take the target of that attack and place him back almost within spitting distance of the place that had served as his home for so long had a humor to it that made the soldier smile. More seriously, it was a case of hide in plain sight, and if security held tight then it would not be the obvious place to search for him.

If security held tight. The last thing Clelland had said to him as he had handed over a piece of paper with the address scribbled on it was to comment that although he had worked hard at establishing contacts and keeping his ear to the ground, it was still obvious that if he had been able to locate the target within the space of a morning, it would not be hard for others to follow suit.

"Mr. Cooper, I don't have to tell you to be cautious, I know that. But I also know that there are so many holes in this cheese that we should be in Switzerland. I'm not sure what I can do to help further, but you know who and where I am. And I can call in some favors. Be sure of that."

"I'll bear that in mind," Bolan had said, grasping the folded scrap. "Who would have thought the old ways would still be the best? Read, memorize, burn or eat. So simple."

"Especially if folded to avoid CCTV. Ironic, isn't it, that the more complex we make communications, the easier it is for the determined to hack into it."

These words still echoed in Bolan's ears as he parked his silver-gray BMW, which looked right at home on these streets. On the backseat was a duffel bag with smoke and concussion grenades, a length of camera cable and a receiver, a night-vision headset, gas mask, a Micro-Uzi and an H&K MP-5, along with the ordnance to keep the SMGs fed. He was traveling light, and on the blacksuit that was concealed beneath the light raincoat he wore he also carried a Desert Eagle in a shoulder holster and a motion-sensor detector.

It was late afternoon. After his meeting with Clelland, he had returned to his office base and checked in with Belinda Hagen. She was not his line manager, but in order to lay down some cover he had told her that his illness was recurring and he was returning home. He had also made a date with her for the following evening, assuring her that she could show him better restaurants than he had so far discovered. It was a low trick to lead her on in one sense, but her enthusiasm would inform any report she should make if his absence was noted and commented on. Anything to deflect attention was a plus.

Returning to the apartment that was his base, his intent had been to freshen up and gather equipment from his improvised hiding place under the closet floorboards. As ever, something for which he thanked Kurtzman's foresight in renting an apartment in an old block that wasn't cursed with concrete or stone floors.

Thinking of Kurtzman reminded him that to check in would be useful. The words of Clelland ringing in his ears, he hit speed dial.

"Secure line?" he asked as Kurtzman's warm tones greeted him.

"As ever," the man replied with some surprise.

"Can't be too sure. Are you?"

"Take my word. Paranoia getting to you?"

"Something like that," Bolan said wearily before filling in Kurtzman on events and requesting schematics for the surveillance area, and any safe houses within the range, which presently sat on his smart phone.

Feeling a little more as if he was back on secured ground after speaking to Kurtzman, he called Grimaldi and had a brief conversation, alerting the flier to his intent and to be on standby.

"Sarge, you know I'm just on the end of speed dial." Grimaldi chuckled. "By the way, I delivered that little package for you safely. And returned the transport. One less thing for you to worry about."

Bolan had been pleased to hear this, though he had never doubted Grimaldi's ability to effect a complete cleanup. If only they had been able to deal with Grozny in the same way as Kowalski.

This was the last thought that ran through his mind as he sat in the BMW, breathing slowly and noting the complete lack of life around the villa three hundred yards from where he had parked.

He exited the vehicle, taking his duffel bag from the backseat and hitting central locking. Might as well make it look the part—it wasn't as if he'd be using the vehicle to leave the scene. He walked along the road, studying the seemingly empty building from the corner of his eye as he passed, and turned the corner.

It looked completely deserted—which was not smart, as even though it was a quiet residential area, all the other buildings at least showed signs of habitation, even if they appeared empty at the moment.

If he could take this in at a glance, he was sure as could be that any other hostile forces could glean the same intel as easily. Would this make his task easier or harder?

Depends how ahead of the game you are, Bolan figured. Hopefully, he was far enough ahead to make the difference.

The house stood in its own grounds, with a driveway and front lawn that had stripes of gravel path, grass and seed beds at the sides. The rear garden would be twice as deep as the front, if the length and depth of the end houses were to be believed.

He took the block at pace, counting until he was standing before the house that backed on to the safe house. There were no alleys or access roads to garages running between, so it would be a matter of going through one piece of land and over a fence into the target area.

The house before him looked empty. Lived in, for sure, but not currently occupied. The gravel driveway was recently cut up by tires, and there was a bicycle under a privet hedge by the left-hand side of the house, leading to a closed door of light wood.

He took the motion-sensor detector and conducted a discreet sweep. Nothing. Not surprising, since it was unlikely that whoever lived here had any notion of what the house at their rear was used for. Most likely, any kind of security would only begin at the perimeter of the two properties. Likely was not certainty, however: the soldier slipped into the front, skirting the driveway and keeping close to what little cover was provided. He shrugged off the raincoat and secreted it beneath a shrub before taking the fiber-optic camera cable from his bag and feeding it over the trellis that ran across the side door. Without snaking it too far and possibly giving away his presence, he had a limited view on the attached monitor, but it was possible to see that the back garden of this house contained a gazebo, and was mostly a well-manicured lawn before a thick bed of shrubs and plants gave way to a back fence lined with trees on the far side.

Not much cover between the side path and the fence, and plenty of places to hide surveillance cams for the safe house.

Enough, though, if he proceeded with caution. Stashing the camera in his duffel bag, he scaled the side entrance and kept close to the house until he reached the back lawn. A closer recce showed that the French windows at the rear of the house looked out over an immaculately manicured lawn, with the presence of an empty paddling pool showing that it was in regular family use. So, best to hope that they stayed out wherever they were for the next half hour or so, then. Even so, Bolan could curse them for being so functional, particularly as he ran the motion-sensor detector over the area before hugging the side fence and making for the far end of the garden.

There was no indication that his presence had been noticed as he huddled into the scant cover provided near the fence. There were motion sensors on the top of the fence, and although he could not see them, he was certain that where there were motion sensors there were also cameras.

That was fine—once over the fence and into the opposition territory he could lay down cover and move quickly. His pressing concern was actually getting over the fence. This should be the most straightforward part of the operation, but the fence was not as simple as it looked. He refrained from touching, as the wire binding the posts and sections of the fencing looked suspiciously as though they were either wired for motion, or to shock. Hunkering down and gently probing the soft earth at the base, he could also see that the posts were rooted deep, founded in concrete. Finally, although it did not go higher than two or two and a half yards tops, the trees were another few feet higher, and their branches did not hang in a manner that would make scaling them a quick, easy matter.

Figuring that there was a chance he would trigger motion sensors and maybe be caught on camera, he opted to use the fiber-optic camera once more, in an attempt to gain some sense of the lay of the land on the other side of the fence.

He made it a rapid recce, as once the camera had been picked up he would need to move swiftly. The foliage on the other side of the fence was dense, but not enough to obscure the view afforded him. The lawn was as well manicured as the one to his rear. It was clear, and he had little doubt that it was pitted with motion-sensor detectors. The back of the house presented a blank and uninviting aspect. There were French windows with heavy drapes across them, and Bolan was almost certain that bars or tripwires would lay behind those drapes. The upper windows appeared equally as impassive, with blinds presenting a blank facade.

The house looked as though it had been built at the same time as the one behind him—the entire block seemed to have come from the same development. In which case, he could assume that there was a side-entrance door into a kitchen or anteroom, much like the one he had passed to get here.

That would be the weak link. Not because it would not be well guarded or armored in some way, but rather because it would be in the most use. Of necessity, therefore, it would have to be less impervious.

He reeled in the camera, stowed it in his duffel bag and, after testing the fence for current and finding it was not wired, ascended rapidly.

The overhanging branches presented a few problems in that they slowed him down. They were dense, and the foliage was tangled. Despite this, he was able to find his footing and slide down the trunk of one until he hit the soft earth. It yielded beneath his feet as he moved out and onto the lawn. No point in scanning for detectors, they would be able to see him. A smoke grenade may have laid down some cover, but it was more important that he did not draw attention to the house. For much the same reason, he doubted that any security would want to come outside and tackle him. From their own surveillance, they would know that he was alone.

So the house would be the battlefield.

He reached the side door, exactly where it was on the corresponding house, and flattened himself against the wall. He had the Micro-Uzi from the duffel bag—short bursts to lay down cover, and only take out any opposition if they were a direct threat. They were not the enemy, even though they would think that of him.

He listened—there was no sound of movement within. The door would either be wired or they would be lying back, waiting.

He cursed the fact that he hadn't packed any explosives,

for to blow the door with a grenade would be wasteful and dangerous in this enclosed passage. There was only one way forward. He moved so that he was at an angle to tap a short burst into the door and kick at it while remaining at an angle that would keep him out of any angle of fire.

The door did not yield immediately, so Bolan sent a second burst into it and kicked again. This time it did swing open. He flattened himself back to the wall, but there was little sign of any habitation.

So that was how they would play it. He entered the house, moving quickly but with caution. He was in a small anteroom that led to the kitchen on one side and a hallway on the other. He could see two doors and a staircase that was open beneath. Recessed was one door, presumably to a basement.

The three doors between the entrance and head of the stairs were taken easily. The basement door crashed back under his boot, with a concussion grenade following. Its detonation blanked any noise made if anyone was in the basement, but by then he had already taken the other two doors, with smoke grenades following. The hallway was filled with billowing clouds of smoke.

Bolan had his gas mask in place, but those guarding the house had not had the foresight, or been quite quick enough. Two men, choking, stumbled through the smoke cover, torn between covering their faces and covering themselves with their weapons. This made them easy to disable.

How many men were in the house? He did not want to assume, but it was possible that he had taken some out in the basement. If you reckoned on a detachment of a half dozen, then it was likely that more than half of them were already out of the game.

He took the stairs looking up, straining for any sound that may give him indications of movement. There was nothing—but this did not mean that he was not under threat.

At the top of the stairs, the passages leading off the landing led to four rooms with closed doors. The bathroom and facilities were visible through two doors that had been left open, with a window—blind down—marking the source of daylight into the passage.

There was no sign of any life whatsoever. Casting a glance down over the handrail of the staircase, he saw that all was quiet below.

Bolan proceeded cautiously, opening each door in turn. There were signs of habitation, but no guards... And no Grozny. The upper floor seemed to be deserted as he opened three of the four doors. Had they somehow got wind of an attack—his or someone else's—and moved the target? Or was this an elaborate blind that Clelland had been suckered into—in which case any cover the young man may have had been effectively blown?

Reaching the last door, Bolan listened. There was the sound of breathing from the far side. More than one man, though one of them was breathing more heavily. He stepped to the side before opening the door.

He was greeted with silence. Bolan paused, nerves on edge but calm enough to play the waiting game.

"You may come in, whoever you are. But carefully. I warn you, I am armed."

Bolan's lips quirked—he recognized the voice. Slowly, holding the Micro-Uzi at a nonthreatening angle, he turned and stood in the doorway.

Two guards lay on the floor, unconscious. Seated on the bed, legs casually crossed, an AK-47 nestled on his lap, Vijas Grozny sniffed appreciatively as he took in the man facing him.

"So, we meet again, as they say. You know, I like your

style, but I have no idea what you want from me. Just that you keep turning up in buildings where I am held prisoner. Which, frankly, is not an everyday occurrence, even in the life I have lived. So, in case we don't get the chance again, tell me—what is your fascination with me, man in black?"

5

From the outside, it would have seemed to any passersby that nothing had occurred within the safe house. The walls were thick and had also been reinforced and soundproofed as part of the security measures taken. More than this, the fact that it was recessed within its own grounds gave it privacy and the necessary distance to kill any sound. Anyone standing where Bolan's car had been parked would have been completely unaware of the conflagration within.

What they would have noticed, however, were the three cars that turned into the street at speed, pulling up before the old house. Two of them flanked the buildings on either side, while the third turned head-on into the driveway before scattering gravel with a hard-braked stop.

The doors of the cars opened—four men emerged from each of the flanking vehicles, and three from the car head-on. Each of the men pulled a ski mask down and inserted nose plugs. The driver of the lead car turned to his men and indicated channels down the side of the house where they should move, finishing with a gesture that made his intention to take down the front door of the house abundantly clear.

To emphasize this, the took a grenade from his pocket and pulled the pin, tossing it underhand in a gentle arc that saw it fall in the recessed porch of the old house. It rolled slowly and came to rest against the door, spinning back only an inch or two before it detonated.

The door, frame and surrounding brickwork disappeared in a haze of smoke, which, as it cleared, showed a twisted metal sheet and frame that revealed further security measures—precautions that had been only partially successful, as the doorway was only partly uncovered.

The lead man roared, half in frustration and half as a rallying cry as he urged the two men with him into the dust cloud, and those at the sides of the buildings into faster action.

Bolan had been deliberate in keeping his actions as undetected as possible—the tactics of these guerrillas were the reverse. They didn't care if they were noticed. Their aim was in then out with the maximum impact and no regard for either visibility or collateral damage.

Which, seeing as they numbered eleven, and there were presently only two men capable of resistance within the walls of the house, could be something of a problem.

A FEW MINUTES earlier, Bolan had removed his gas mask so that the recumbent Grozny could see his face.

"A good job," the soldier commented mildly, indicating the incapacitated guards. "Care to share why?"

Grozny shrugged. "Trust. A simple matter. I have none."

"Then should I expect a standoff with you?"

Grozny chuckled. "Perhaps. But you are different. You are working with these people but are not one of them. It is an interesting stance and one that I find intriguing. You are for hire? A mercenary, perhaps?"

Bolan shook his head. "That's the last thing I am. But you are right in one thing—I work with these people at the moment, but I'm not with them. There are holes all over the security of the International War Crimes Tribunal. My job is to make sure you reach trial."

"And these," Grozny interjected, "that was their objective, apparently."

"I wouldn't doubt their integrity," Bolan said crisply, "but I might doubt the integrity of those who know they are here. Best if we operate on a need-to-know basis on this one. That's why I made sure they only had superficial wounds, just to put them out of the game."

"Considerate of you—not so considerate with the Serbs who rescued me from incarceration. I seem to recall that most of them are now resting six feet beneath the ground."

"I didn't put them all there," Bolan murmured. "I think you know that."

Grozny laughed; a low rumble that ended in a cough. "I have some issues with those who would seek to put me on a pedestal. I ask myself where they were for the two decades that I was in hiding."

"Looking for you like the war crimes commission, maybe?"

Grozny shrugged. "Perhaps… But I still keep my ear to the ground, and I know they were a nothing organization. A splinter of a splinter. No money, no friends and no credibility. So where do they suddenly get the resources to mount such a raid? Why do they come to me out of nowhere, when until a year ago they never so much as mentioned me? The idea of escaping prison was appealing, but what would come afterward? Maybe not so much…"

"You think that they wouldn't install you as president of their new state?"

Grozny chuckled again. "I might be installed, but would I serve?"

"Interesting thinking. So what are your options?"

"Perhaps—"

Bolan never got to hear those options. At that moment an earsplitting roar echoed from the front of the house.

THE THREE SERBS hammered their way through the metal sheeting and were into the hallway. Down the side entrance that Bolan had left open, four men entered, but not without hesitation at how easy it was. On the far side, the four men allocated to that area made their way down the blank wall running along the building and round to the back garden. Here they came up against the closed French windows. Unaware of the ease with which their colleagues were making progress, they wasted little time in blasting the doors open with bursts of fire from their BXP-10 SMGs. The drapes, shredded by the ordnance, revealed the heavy metal grille beyond, which was taken out by blasts at the corners, tearing hinges.

Wisps of smoke from the grenades loosed by Bolan a few minutes before still lingered in the air, and caused the Serbs to falter, momentarily taken aback by the lack of resistance and the uncanny quiet as their own fire died away.

The four men who had taken the side entrance, and those from the rear of the house, had visual contact. Exchanged glances and shrugs revealed their confusion. The three men who had entered by the front then came into view. The heavyset man who was their leader—and who knew more than any of them the true meaning of this attack—gestured to them to take the rooms on the ground floor, and also for two of them to venture down to the basement past the ruined doorway.

While four of the men scoped the rooms on the ground floor and found them deserted, the two who descended to the basement found a scene that took them by surprise. The room had housed the comms and surveillance equipment for the house, but which was presently out of operation, while three men lay unconscious on the floor, their seats scattered across the bare boards. They were breathing, but were out cold.

More confused than before, the two Serbs hurried back up the stairs until they were in the hallway, where their confused glances met with those of their companions, all equally unsure of what had occurred.

Their leader, at the foot of the stairs, had more of an idea. Scowling, he indicated that most of them stay back, while gesturing for two to join him. He had little doubt that the hand behind this was the same as had taken out his men the last time they had secured their target.

This time, his men would be ready.

GROZNY HAD BEEN on his feet, the AK-47 in a stance that habit had allowed him to easily slip into, moving toward the window and flattening himself beside it, staring out to the street beyond. Bolan had moved across to the doorway, stepping out into the hallway, leading with the Micro-Uzi. Despite the earsplitting detonation, his hearing was still clear enough to discern the footsteps that pounded through the floor below. They weren't being subtle, and were obviously in a hurry, but nonetheless would be slowed by surprise at their lack of resistance.

The question was this: what would their next move be? Would they have more caution, or could he expect a rapid frontal assault?

Moving back into the bedroom where Grozny was leaving his position by the window, the two men came together and spoke in hushed, rapid tones.

"Three cars out front, one in the drive. Unless they're expert, which I doubt, the amateurs have left no one on guard."

"Planning on a quick hit," Bolan murmured. "In, out,

and no need to watch your back…. Figure we can get down the front of the building?"

Grozny shook his head. "No footholds, besides I can't do that shit since my leg went ten years back. The only way I can do this is to go through them."

"Great," Bolan said grimly. "It's about three, maybe four, to one."

Grozny gave a vulpine grin that was more of a sneer. "I took out twenty men once, so—"

"Save it. You'll need all the breath you have." And when Grozny looked quizzical, Bolan added, "You'll see. Just follow me. We're going to have to be as subtle as the enemy. Maybe less so…"

THE HEAVYSET SERB took a smoke grenade from the pocket of his combat jacket. With only nose plugs and no goggles, he couldn't risk CS with his own men. He was at a disadvantage heading up the stairs, which made an easy target for anyone nestling at the top. On the other hand, in a building like this there was no other way out, and considering the guards they knew of had been taken out of the equation, there was only one man they were likely to be facing. Unless Grozny opted to side with him—something that the heavyset Serb would not have found surprising.

He primed the grenade, carrying his BXP-10 nestled in the crook of his arm, and started to ascend the stairs slowly, listening for any indication of life from above. At his back, the second man followed, gulping down his fear as the sweat prickled his brow. The adrenaline from a full-on assault had been replaced by trepidation at something unexpected, and the tension was telling on him. He risked a look down to where the rest of the Serbs waited. They looked about as confident as he felt.

Risking that look meant that the second man missed the

moment when the concussion grenade hit the stair carpet at his feet with a dull thud, rolling against the toe of his boot.

He looked stupidly at it, and then at his leader. The heavyset Serb opened his mouth to yell, but before any sound could escape he was obliterated from his compatriot's view by the detonation of the concussion grenade.

BOLAN COULD SENSE, rather than see, that the enemy had started their ascent. Their caution was what he would have expected, and it played right into his hands. He primed the grenade and gently lobbed it over the stair rail before stepping back into the doorway of the bedroom, pushing Grozny back so they were both within the room before he pushed the door shut and opened his mouth to equalize pressure, gesturing that the aging warlord do the same. Grozny, realizing what Bolan's tactic was, quickly complied as the grenade detonated beneath them. The concussion below made the floor shake below them.

Bolan indicated to the warlord that he follow, acknowledged by a nod from Grozny, before pulling the door open and heading for the top of the stairs. The grenade should—in the enclosed space of the hallway below—have taken out anyone who was in the vicinity. The only problem would be if any of the invading party had been in a separate part of the house.

Time to worry about that later. Flicking the switch on the Micro-Uzi so that it was on rapid fire, Bolan came down the stairs with his back to the wall. The bottom was obscured in smoke and the bodies of two men. One had taken the full force of the blast, and the heavier man lying a yard from him had been shielded enough to still be alive, if out of action.

As he descended, Grozny a few feet apart and with his own AK-47 trained into dangerous spaces, the soldier opened fire with a spray 'n' pray pattern that was intended to take out anyone within range or drive them back.

Beyond the heavyset man's prone body lay the open front doorway, a mass of twisted metal and splintered wood, but with enough of a gap not to slow them down. Which was good. Because despite Bolan's own efforts at unobtrusiveness, the arrival of the Serbs and his need to get past them would no doubt have raised an alarm that would have a Koninklijke detachment speeding toward them even as the thought crossed his mind.

His own car sat just a couple of hundred yards down the road. If they could make that without being impeded, they had a chance of getting away.

Bolan made the bottom of the stairs and hit the floor, using the bodies of the two prone men as cover. He took in that the passage to the rear of the house was littered with men who had been taken out by the concussion grenade. If there was anyone left standing, they were concealing themselves.

This was a suspicion that was confirmed by the chatter of a BXP-10 and the smack of shells into the plasterwork and wood of the wall behind and above him.

He cursed to himself. Dealing with this would waste precious seconds. He laid down a suppressing fire and felt for a smoke grenade. No time to flush out and eliminate the remaining enemy—only enough to stop them from firing on Grozny and himself as they exited the scene.

The aging warlord, seeing what Bolan was doing, moved his own position so that although he was shielded from fire emanating from the back of the passage, he was able to get enough of an angle to fire back far enough to take chunks out of the wall near the doorways to the back room and the cellar, on either side of the hall.

Bolan, appreciative of the assistance, ceased his own fire

as he fished out the smoke grenade and primed it before rolling it over the bodies providing his cover, and along the hallway. As it detonated and laid down a thick blanket, he could hear the sound of one man struggling to breathe, despite the nose plugs that he must be wearing.

Rising to a crouch, Bolan laid down a suppressing burst. Grozny moved down to the foot of the stairs and gestured for Bolan to move out, taking over the bursts of fire as he did so.

Out in the clean air, Bolan could see that the immediate area was deserted—Grozny had been correct in his assessment. Yet, Bolan still moved to the end of the driveway and the gateway with caution. In the distance he could hear sirens.

Despite the carnage behind Bolan, and the approaching police force, the area was still quiet, suburban and deserted. It was incongruous, and yet it would allow them to get to his car with alacrity.

Looking back, he beckoned to Grozny, who was backing out of the doorway. With a final blast of covering fire, the aging warlord turned and strode across the driveway until he was at Bolan's side.

The soldier indicated his car. "Keep it frosty, Grozny. We don't want any innocent bystanders caught up in this."

"My friend, I do not want anyone caught up in this, innocent or otherwise. I just want to get away."

The two men moved out into the street and made their way toward the car. Bolan was acutely aware of the encroaching sirens, and also of the fact that they were completely exposed in this suburban street. The quiet now seemed unnatural. There must be some people who were home, and if so, they had elected to stay out of the way while a firefight happened on their doorstep. Bolan was relieved—the last thing he wanted was to have to deal with some well-meaning but misinformed passerby.

As they approached the car he remembered that he had hit the central locking. With no intention of having to use the car again, he wasn't sure if he had left the keys in the raincoat, which still lay under a bush around the block. But it was with no little relief that he found them as they were on top of the car, and so was not forced to risk noticeable damage in effecting entry.

Grozny slid into the front passenger seat beside Bolan as the soldier hit the ignition and put the vehicle into drive. He put the AK-47 out of view as Bolan pulled out into the road and tossed the duffel bag on the backseat.

"I take it that we will be headed in the opposite direction to the sirens," Grozny queried.

"Absolutely. And I'll be sticking to the speed limit religiously."

"Of course. I take it this was not your original plan?"

Bolan shook his head. "No worries. I can return to that once we evac the immediate area. It'd be a shame to tangle with the good guys."

"You know who they are?" Grozny asked with ill-disguised humor.

"Mostly. The real question is—do you? Did you ever?"

Grozny's disgruntled silence in response came as a relief as the soldier took the car away from the scene and the onrushing police.

THE SAFE HOUSE was toward the south of Den Haag and took them just over an hour to reach, Bolan making sure that they hadn't picked up a tail at any point. It was unlikely, but an outside possibility if anyone in the suburbs had noted the make or license plate of the car. Not wanting to leave himself open to being traced via an unsecured line, the soldier refrained from calling Grimaldi. The ace pilot had been on standby, and expecting a call. Bolan knew that he would be itchy, wondering if something had gone wrong. Despite this, the soldier elected to maintain silence.

They pulled up in a poorer area of town, where blocks of apartments erected in the 1980s replaced the elegant town houses of the area they had recently vacated. This was more akin to the area where Grozny had been taken after the prison break, and the warlord smiled as he got out of the car.

"Back to where it started. Who would think of looking for us here?"

"That's the idea," Bolan said shortly. "Follow me."

He led Grozny through the courtyard of one block, reaching the back entry. They ascended two flights of emergency stairs before coming out to a balcony walkway that was littered with trash bags and children's bikes and toys. At the far end of the walkway was a steel-shuttered door on an apartment that showed every sign of being deserted. Checking if they were being overlooked, Bolan took the key to the shutter padlock and removed it, allowing them access.

"This is very impressive," Grozny said as Bolan secured the door behind them and flicked the light switch, revealing that the apartment was far from derelict. It was sparsely furnished, with a sofa and two armchairs facing a TV and coffee table in one room; a bed and cabinet in each of the two bedrooms; a bathroom equipped with toiletries; and a kitchen that held a well-stocked refrigerator and pantry.

"It is," Bolan replied in an impassive tone. Grimaldi had been busy—one of his tasks had been to prepare this apartment for after the snatch, and he had made sure that they had no need to leave until the day Grozny's trial began. While the warlord admired the interior of the apartment and foraged for food, Bolan busied himself checking the security measures that Grimaldi had taken. The windows were covered by metal shutters much like the door, to create the impression of dereliction. However, each of the shutters on the apartment had small spy holes set in them with fish-eye lenses. On the inside, the glass had been removed from the windows to prevent any damage or injury from shattering, should they come under attack.

In one bedroom, Grimaldi had left some ordnance to boost that which Bolan had carried with him. Alongside the bags containing this was an unregistered cell phone that had been loaded with scrambling software and a program to jam scanners and so prevent a pinpointing of position. Bolan knew this to be the case, as it had been one of his instructions, and he knew that Kurtzman had downloaded the software for Grimaldi to install.

Glad that he could finally deal with some business, Bolan hit the speed dial for Grimaldi that the flier had inserted in the cell.

"Sarge, where the hell are you?" Grimaldi said immediately on answering. "I was waiting for your call, then picked up a Koninklijke transmission. Jeez, those guys must love you."

"I'm on their Christmas-card list, Jack." Bolan grinned before outlining what had happened to deflect from their original plan and lead him to this point. He finished up. "Nice job you've done, Jack. We should be okay here until the trial. Check in every six, and we'll liaise about getting him to court in one piece."

"Sure thing, Sarge. Say, you going to call Hal?"

"I'm going to have to. Any reason?"

Grimaldi chuckled. "I'd love to be able to listen in on that one, that's all."

"Sure you don't want to make it for me? I wouldn't mind," Bolan retorted with a humor he didn't really feel.

And sure enough, when he spoke to the big Fed, Brognola was far from pleased.

"I thought you understood the meaning of subtle, Striker! Hellfire, how much of the Hague do you want to lay waste?"

"Hal, it wasn't down to me. I was in there without anyone noticing until the Serbs turned up. They're the ones who don't do subtle."

"I'll take your word for it. Believe me, I'm taking your heat."

"Yeah, well, someone is getting big money to make sure that Grozny is found. And not for his health, either. They want a martyr, they want to make it look like it's crossfire and they don't want him to get to trial before it all happens. Most important, they don't care if they make a big noise over it."

Brognola cursed softly. "Who can we trust?"

"No one. Not even Clelland. I like him, but we can't guarantee he's being tracked without knowing. Leave it to me. I'll get our boy his day in court."

"Okay. Take it easy out there, Striker. I'll keep the heat off from my end. I never did mind getting my ass burned, anyway."

"That's just as well," Bolan said. It was only when he disconnected that he realized that Grozny was in the doorway, listening to him while demolishing a sandwich.

"Hungry. Fighting makes you that way," the warlord said. "You should eat, too. It's been a long time for me since I had the gnawing hunger that follows battle."

"I'll fix something later," Bolan replied. "I have things to do first."

Grozny snorted. "So there is no one I can trust, eh?

Except maybe you. Except maybe that I don't even know you. But yes, I think I can. I think you are like me, a man of principle."

Bolan eyed him coldly. "That kind of depends on the principles," was all he said.

6

The two men passed each other outside the International Criminal Tribunal for the former Yugoslavia. A studious Chinese tourist with his guidebook and a heavyset Serb with a limp and the look of someone who had been in a bar fight. They passed the building on the sidewalk that lay across the busy road from the building's entrance.

As they crossed paths, the Chinese man dropped his guidebook, and the Serb bent down to pick it up—a random act of kindness as he handed it back.

"Thank you," Xiao Li said simply. "You have had an accident?"

"Funny. You're a funny man, anyone ever say that to you? I'd be really surprised if they had."

"Such bitter sentiments are uncalled for. Would you care for coffee? Personally, I don't drink it, but you Westerners are all the same. 'Mad for it,' I believe is the term."

The Serb scowled. "I don't like you when you're in a good mood. I don't know why you should be, given that we fucked up again. I'd be furious. I am furious, if it comes to it. And I get jumpy when we meet in the open, in a place like this."

"'Hide in plain sight' is another of your phrases from the media of which I am fond," Xiao commented. "I want you to take a good look at this place, as the next time you see it, you will be leading an assault on it."

The Serb stared—it was all he could do not to laugh with disdain. "You're a fucking madman," he stated simply.

Xiao's face did not betray the amusement he felt inside. "Perhaps, but perhaps not. If you allow me to outline a possible course of action for you, which I have already taken the liberty of assuming you will agree with, then you may change your mind."

The Serb's brow furrowed. "After the beating we've got from that bastard in black and with the Koninklijke up our ass, I'd say we don't have much choice."

BOLAN FELT LIKE climbing the walls. Thirty-six hours in a cell—for that was what this safe house was, after all—with the aging warlord, and he was nearly at the point where he could happily turn him over to anyone who wanted him.

The thing that grated was the assumption on Grozny's part that he and the soldier were cut from the same cloth. Maybe that was true in a certain sense. Both men had been soldiers for their country, and had believed in that nation and its values, and both men had fought willingly for those beliefs. But that was where the similarity ended.

Bolan did not believe in the sanctity of human life—how could he? The number of men he had dispatched over the years made that clear. Yet each of them had been engaged in practices that had been designed to ruin and destroy lives. Whether those practices had been fueled by political ideology or by the desire for power and cash, the result had been the same. Innocent people had been killed, maimed or tortured. By taking out the source of that destruction, he had sought to save more innocent lives. The concept of "the greater good" underpinned his actions.

Grozny, feeling secure in his own monstrous ego and

the misplaced belief in their similarities, had been—almost compelled, it seemed—to discuss the things he had done during the war of 1992-1995, and how his idealism had driven him on.

The only respite the soldier had from the warlord was when he undertook his nightly recce of the immediate area. Leaving the apartment under cover of night, he secured the front so that Grozny was contained, then climbed to the roof of the apartment building. Grimaldi had chosen it with one eye on the surround, as the roof gave an excellent vantage point to all points of the compass. There were no buildings on a higher level within half a mile, and much of the surround was low-level storefronts and empty lots. Even in the early hours, there were still gangs of youths milling about, but the small-time hoods and petty drug dealers plying their trade, along with those who kept them in ready cash, presented no threat. The temptation to take out his anger and frustration by cleaning up the neighborhood was strong, but the knowledge of the attention this would bring to bear stayed his hand.

He contented himself by taking notes—filming the dealers and hoods along with their clientele on the equipment that he used to scour the area, and building a record to hand over to the local lower-level law enforcement agencies via Gordon Clelland once this situation had been resolved. It would have to be through a third party. Even if his identity was still unknown, his actions would hardly make him persona grata with the locals.

This activity, along with the recce, served also to take his mind off what he heard from the mouth of the warlord. He recalled the defense of Karadzic at his trial—that he was a leader of his people and every action was a defense against the injustices that had been perpetrated against them: a marking of parameters to make sure that it never happened again. Bolan had little doubt from what had come out of Grozny's mouth that he would spew the same line.

It seemed odd that this man, who had spent so many years on the run as a mercenary and then making another identity for himself in order to escape capture and trial should find it so easy to yield to the notion of court and possible incarceration. Part of it, perhaps, was bowing to the inevitable: if he could not regain his freedom and the anonymity that had served him for so long, then at least he would have the opportunity to explain himself to the world and proclaim the beliefs that he had been forced to keep inside for so long. Another part—and of this Bolan was certain—was down to the pragmatic qualities of the man. The same instinct that had told him when to walk away and hide nearly two decades before had again kicked in regarding his current situation.

The choice was simple. Go to trial, and if nothing else, he would still have life. Yield to the separatist group who had made the bid to free him, and the chances are he would end up a dead national hero. If their aims succeeded—otherwise, just dead. How would that profit him? Once he was dead, it didn't matter.

Did any of it? While part of Bolan's mind was focused on the recce of the immediate area, there were things that had been said that still gnawed at the back of his head.

Such as the villages that had been taken over by Grozny's men and set up as rape camps, where the women were forced to reproduce a pure strain of Serb. The women were impregnated by the invading forces in what was presented as a scientific process but was little more than a way of keeping the fighting men sweet by giving them their jollies. The way in which all such so-called noble aims were discarded when the enemy was at the door of the camps were wiped out, purged by fire as though that would destroy the knowledge and memory of what had been done.

The so-called ethnic cleansing that had seen whole communities decimated of anyone whose origins were less than a hundred percent verifiable in an effort to make sure that the homeland being established was one that had a mythical purity to it—genocide for the sake of a genetic myth.

The casual everyday cruelty toward the civilians caught in the crossfire of the war. Of course, civilians suffered when forces invaded, but this was far more than that: torture and killing for pleasure and to establish your own sense of superiority.

That was war, but it was not Bolan's idea of war. War was what happened when you had no option. To Grozny, war was what happened when you didn't get your own way. Like a spoiled child—but a strong, dangerous and ultimately stupid child.

Reining in his own personal distaste, allowing the solitude of the recce to wash over him, Bolan knew that his mission would see the best of a series of unsatisfactory outcomes. Grozny would live, but he would live in captivity, locked away from the world he had contaminated. A world that would hopefully see his views for the twisted garbage they were, and that would despise or pity rather than sympathize with him. As an example to anyone who had the idiocy to think the same way, perhaps?

Bolan left his post and climbed down to the balcony walkway, letting himself back into the apartment before securing it once more.

"Any sign of action?" Grozny asked when he saw him.

"Just the local scum rising to the surface. Nothing else to cause a ripple," Bolan replied.

"A poetic soldier," Grozny commented. "A noble tradition. I, myself, had no time for such things. I am not a man of words. I am a man of action. I would not have marked you down as a poetic man, Cooper. Your actions seem to speak louder, if you will allow. Better to plan a campaign that will bring the enemy to their knees than to write a poem that will impress their women. It makes me think of—"

Bolan took a deep breath. There was nothing he could say or do that would halt the ceaseless flow of words from the warlord. It was as though the man had held his silence for so long in his need to stay underground that he could not resist the audience that was presently confined with him.

Bolan would be glad when this was over. He'd even almost welcome the distraction of an attack at this moment.

XIAO AND THE SERB guerrilla had made their way a few blocks to a Starbucks. The same one that Clelland used every day, and where he had met with Bolan. For the young American it was a piece of home. For the Oriental diplomat it was a chance to exercise his sense of humor without necessarily revealing it to his superiors, where it would not gain approval.

It was therefore fortunate for the young American, and not so for the Oriental, that Clelland was indulging his daily habit when he saw the two men enter. He was fairly certain that they did not know who he was: conversely, he recognized the Serb from the description Bolan—via Brognola—had given him, and the Oriental from the photograph contained in his files.

The Serb he had identified as Miro Millevich. A known nationalist activist condemned by the right as being hotheaded and inclined to violence. Ostracized by those with whom he held sympathy. He had been on surveillance lists, but had dropped off the map some time before. But finally he'd reappeared, looking the worse for wear and obviously back in the game. That explained a lot—as did the presence of the diplomat who had previous ties with Grozny.

This seemed to add two and two and come up with a nice even four. Clelland could make an educated guess at what the two men were discussing, but caught without any surveillance tech, he could do nothing to get closer and glean details. It was frustrating for him. All, however, was not lost.

From the corner of his eye, the young American could watch them from his position. He tried to lip-read, to pick up anything he could by way of a clue. But the Serb had a heavy accent that affected his pronunciation, and the Oriental barely moved his lips as he spoke. The effect was little more than frustrating.

The one thing that did catch Clelland's attention, though, was the way in which the Oriental tapped on his cell and then indicated that the Serb look to his own. Certainly, something passed between them, and if that was so and they had numbers for either phone in their intel, then a hack could be effected.

Not much, admittedly, but perhaps the kind of break he needed. Just to stumble on this was fortune enough.

Clelland finished his coffee and got up to leave. He was careful not to look in the direction of the Serb and the Oriental as he exited, steering himself as far away from them as was possible without undue ostentation.

It was only when he was outside, and half a block away, sure that he could not be observed—even by accident—that he took his own cell from his jacket and hit speed dial for the scrambled line that Brognola had given him.

"Mr. Brognola? It's Gordon Clelland. I have something that I think you and Mr. Cooper should know about…."

GROZNY WAS A news junkie. The safe-house apartment had a TV and cable feed. Bolan was wary of it being in use, as the signal could cause them to be traced. It was unlikely, given the amount of cable feeds in this district alone, and the fact that the group attempting a trace were hardly the most resourced or efficient, but nonetheless the atmosphere of Den Haag since his arrival had engendered a paranoia in him that was higher than usual.

Besides, faced with the prospect of having to listen to another of the warlord's interminable and sickening tales, the slim-chance risk of being traced was one Bolan was prepared to take. There was a part of him that felt as though any more comparisons between the warlord and himself, and he might be tempted to do the Serb's job for them. It was only a passing thought, but the soldier wanted to remain focused, and if that entailed allowing Grozny to feed his habit, then so be it.

The warlord had a routine that was quickly established. Rise early, exercise—he had a regime worked out for confinement, originating as it had in prison—and then settle down before the TV to start flicking between the news channels that were available. A couple of hours of this, then more exercise before eating and returning to the TV, climaxing in a final burst of physical activity before turning in as Bolan commenced his nightly recce.

It had been only a couple of days, but it had seemed to stretch out for an eternity. An eternity of Fox and Sky News; Canal Plus and the BBC; Al Jazeera in Arabic and English; Russia Today—the list was endless. Grozny preferred them to the Dutch, German and Spanish channels that were also available. His polyglot tendencies were similar to Bolan's—a smattering of many languages picked up through experience, but only a few that could be considered fluent enough to provide cover. For all the channels, the warlord would flick restlessly, muttering a running commentary on how the same stories occurring on each channel were angled to the ideologies—usually those he disdained. For those stories that were covered only by some channels he would comment bitterly on how information was kept from the peoples of that land.

For the most part, Bolan blotted this out as he went about his business. There were preparations to be made, as the trial was presently only a day from commencement.

"Jack, is this a secure line?"

"Sarge, if this isn't secured then I'm going to string Bear up by his chair from under Dragonslayer and take him for a little ride."

"The Bear seal of approval, eh? I'll take that one," Bolan said. It was good to hear a friendly voice in this self-imposed prison. "Countdown is less than twenty-fours, and we need to arrange cover. I'm taking Grozny in, and I'll need you to sort out transport. Did you arrange disposal?"

"Sarge, that vehicle was gone before you even had time to get the coffee brewing. No way it could be traced to your location. I can get you an olive-green Saab, key taped under the rear fender, at the same location by 07:45 tomorrow. Can't tell you the plates as I haven't had them replaced yet, but I can confirm that tonight."

"That's what I like to hear. I don't know if they plan to hit us before we go in, or when we're inside, but I'm accounting for both eventualities. I want you to have Dragonslayer ready to hit the air as soon as you hear from me. I might need the backup, or I might need an evac."

"I'll be ready for both. You heard anything from the big man?"

"Not yet. I think I'm going to have to call him myself… after I speak to Bear."

"You speak to him you might not need the big man. If there's anything to know."

"I'm hoping there'll be nothing and it'll all go smoothly."

"You don't joke much, Sarge, but when you do…" Jack chuckled. "Let me get on to the vehicle for you, and I'll be ready and waiting tomorrow."

Bolan disconnected, and paused before calling Stony Man Farm. He could hear Al Jazeera in Arabic from the next room. Even with his rudimentary grasp of Arabic he could understand that it was a story about Grozny's upcoming trial, and his seclusion. He could hear a representative of the Koninklijke explaining that the prisoner had been parceled to a safe house and was under surveillance for his own safety until the trial. His mouth quirked—how much would the Koninklijke like to run him out of the Netherlands? he wondered.

"Bear, speak to me," he said as his speed dial was an immediate pickup.

"Striker, I wonder if by any chance that's Al Jazeera I can pick up in the background?"

"That's very good sound filtering you have there."

"Ah, I thought so. Have you been able to catch what they've just been talking about?"

"Some of it. I would guess that, by the way they're lying through their teeth, the locals have been briefed about what's going down—at least on a need to know. And I'd also hazard a guess that they're not too happy."

"Correct on both counts. The big man has called in a few favors to exert a little pressure and stop them looking too hard and trampling all over any trails we might find. It's just made them madder than they were. They've not been big fans of yours since the PIH breakout."

"I can see why not, but I was just doing what I had to. What they should have been doing. But as long as they give me a clear path tomorrow… I've made arrangements with Jack and I'll deliver the goods right to the courtroom myself. Once the trial begins, it's up to them and their holding facilities. I figure the Serbs will make one last push."

"You figure it'll be that?" Kurtzman quizzed. "Reasons?"

"One—to make a push at that point will probably shoot their bolt. They must be a hell of a lot of men down, and even if they are being bankrolled by outside sources, once the trial begins their reason for paying goes out the window. Added to that, they want a martyr who has been hard done by—the crap that's going to hit during that trial won't help them in the long run."

"So we get through tomorrow—rather, you get through tomorrow—and it's mission accomplished."

"Exactly. What would really help are schematics of the routes into the court building, and any underground access—sewers, tunneling, anything—that can clue me in to a possible ingress and also give me some escape routes."

"I can scare that up for you in the next hour and send it through. Is there anything else I can do for you, Striker?"

"You heard anything from the big man? I'm short on local intel."

"Nothing that's come through us here," Kurtzman mused. "Which means it's either all quiet, or Hal needs to speak to you about it himself."

"Then I guess he's the next call on my list," Bolan said. He was certain that the enemy would not miss this chance, and the lack of intel was worrying more than reassuring under those circumstances.

As Kurtzman disconnected, Bolan sat looking at his smart phone, wondering what the requested schematics would reveal. If it could give him the glimmer of any possible weak spots, then that would be an immeasurable help. But not as much as some solid intel.

The cell rang. He was momentarily surprised, all the

more so when he noted that it was an unrecognized number. If this device had been traced or hacked, then…but Kurtzman's software was as good as it gets. He elected to answer warily.

"Mr. Cooper? This is Gordon Clelland. I've been speaking to Mr. Brognola and he suggested I call you."

"On an unscrambled line?" Bolan asked with incredulity.

"He made me install some kind of app he sent me first, so I'm guessing not," Clelland replied with assurance. "I think he felt I should speak to you directly."

"Then speak," Bolan said simply.

Clelland outlined what had happened to him that morning, and what had occurred after his discussion with Brognola. From the digging put into operation by the big Fed, it seemed that the two cells involved could not easily be traced, and the chances of finding out what had been sent between them were slim to nothing.

"At least we know they're planning something," Bolan said at length. "As long as I can put provisional measures in place—"

"We may know more than that, Mr. Cooper," Clelland cut in. "I've called in a few favors of my own. You don't work here long before that kind of opportunity opens itself up to you. There are two things that might be important. One is that the traffic-signal system in the area surrounding the court has been scheduled for maintenance. This means it will be taken off its centralized database and locally controlled by mechanics. It's only four months since the last routine inspection, and this is a mite quicker than usual. The second thing is that the roster system for the guards inside the court has had several changes over the last two days. Men calling in sick, or swapping duty days with colleagues. Now, I know this kind of thing happens, but when you analyze the trend, it's forty percent up on a usual week. Take the two together, and I get kind of suspicious."

"That sounds like a reasonable conclusion," Bolan said quietly. "You're a good man, Gordon, and when I'm through with this I owe you a latte, or something stronger. It'd be good to buy you that."

"It would be my pleasure, Mr. Cooper."

As they exchanged farewells and Bolan disconnected, his mind raced—the traffic signals could cause the kind of jam that would make Grozny a sitting target. The roster changes could bring in ringers or bought men. It gave Bolan something to plan against, but made it no clearer whether the attack would be from outside or within.

Either way, it was going to be one hell of a trip.

7

"This time we shall not fail. We cannot. It is not just that we need this man, it is that we need the money that we are getting in order to fulfill our destiny."

The heavyset Serb, leader of the cell by default as he was the most senior left alive, gathered his men around him. They were depleted in number, but as he looked across the eight faces that were arrayed before him, he felt a surge of pride and hope. There were three brothers and a cousin among the eight, and they were the children of men who had served under Grozny. They carried with them the zeal of their fathers, and he knew they would lay down their lives willingly. The other five ranged from twenty-two to fifty, and although the older men had less physical prowess than their younger compatriots, they had served their time in the war and had experience they could bring.

Maybe with a smaller, tighter force he could effect that which had proved beyond him before this. If nothing else, they had a tight arena of attack, and the cash of the Chinese to grease the wheels.

"I want you to look at this," he said, bringing up the schematics of the road system around the court on the iPad that sat on the table around which they were clustered. He indicated the key areas as he spoke.

"We have the traffic-control system in our hands. Money

is a wonderful tool, and almost as wonderful as this…" He picked up a cable-and-box system that held a keypad and readout. "These are the manual controls used to test the traffic-control points. Thanks to our friends, we have a scheduled maintenance run that takes the points off the central grid. We will tap into the system here, here and here," he added, indicating a nexus of avenues that formed a triangle around the block housing the court building.

"We gridlock the existing traffic so that air is the only way in. But even then they will have to drop men down, and the buildings are clustered so tight that this will prove difficult. Any way you look at it, this buys us time."

"Time is all very well," one of the older men muttered, his lined and thin face reflecting his worn and weary years of experience, "but what do we do with this time?"

"First we make sure that Grozny and that fucker in the blacksuit are inside the catchment area. Then we mount attacks here and here," he continued, indicating two separate points, one of which caused the older man to raise an eyebrow.

"There?"

The Serb leader grinned. "They won't know what hit them. No way will they suspect this…"

BOLAN WAS AWAKE before the sun came up. There was preparation to be done before they set out, and he wanted to get as much of it done as possible before the aging warlord awoke and began one of his interminable monologues.

Ordnance for the day—Micro-Uzi and Desert Eagle, along with sufficient inventory for each. Some C-4 and detonators—offhand he couldn't think of a situation where he might need them, but he wanted to cover even the eventualities he could not imagine. There was no way he would be caught out this close to the post.

Benchmade Stryker automatic knife with four-inch Tanto blade—this he sheathed in the small of his back. It could have a number of uses. A Benelli M-3T combat shotgun with a folding stock: auto and pump action, with a seven-rounds tube and one chambered, each holding double 0 buckshot at twenty-seven .33-calibre pellets per round. It was a destructive and indiscriminate weapon in a confined space, but one that may have its uses nonetheless.

Finally, he gathered concussion and CS grenades, plus a gas mask and a monocular night-vision headset with infrared and heat functions. This latter may prove unnecessary, but again he was trying to go outside the box and cover even those situations he could not imagine.

Almost as an afterthought, he packed a spare gas mask for Grozny. It wouldn't do to have the warlord delivered to court with eyes streaming, coughing up parts of lung.

Standing back from the bed, where he had laid out the tools, he ran a weather eye over them. There was enough here to cover just about anything and still be mobile. He loaded up the blacksuit and put the rest into a duffel bag for ease of conveyance. There was only one more thing he needed to check. He took out his cell and called the unrecognized number stored from the previous day.

When Clelland answered he sounded like someone roused from sleep—looking at his watch, Bolan realized this was probably the case.

"Gordon, it's Cooper. I need you to check something for me."

"Mr. Cooper, sir… Give me one second." Clelland's voice betrayed his struggle to snap out of sleep. Bolan waited. He could hear something that sounded like splashing, and then Clelland came back on line, clearer. "Sorry, sir, you caught me out. What can I do for you?"

"I need to know if the guard will be expecting me to

deliver to the tradesman's entrance as per all prisoners, and at what time. If I turn up and I'm not expected, then it could cause problems."

"It could cause problems, anyway, Mr. Cooper, if some of those roster changes have been bought."

"I realize that, but *that* I can deal with if it arises. What I don't want is a breakdown of communication to get honest men—or me, come to that—in the firing line unnecessarily."

"Understood. I know the signal went out as I tracked that for Mr. Brognola. I don't know if it has reached the right level untainted, but I can make some calls and find out. I will have the answer for you in fifteen, if you can wait."

"That would be fine, Gordon. I'll wait to hear from you."

After disconnecting the call, Bolan could hear that Grozny was awake. The warlord coughed heavily and hawked before muttering to himself. The soldier could hear him make his ablutions as he finished his own preparations, and by the time he was in the living room, placing the duffel bag on one of the easy chairs, the warlord was in the kitchen, brewing up coffee.

"You want some? Get some caffeine into your system. Like amphetamines but without the bad health effects. Unless you're my doctor, in which case you tell me that it is bad for the heart. Pity no one told him that I do not have a heart, eh?"

"Pity is something you know a lot about, right? Especially when it concerns yourself," Bolan replied.

"Easy for you to say," Grozny snapped. "You are not about to go to court and have your character assassinated by some group of idiot lawyers who have no idea about warfare."

"Better for you if it's just your character that's assassinated, and not the rest of you," Bolan said shortly.

"It is a shame that you feel this way," Grozny said sadly. "I felt that we had some affinity."

Bolan could still not believe what he was hearing. Grozny had been a good soldier in some respects, but had overstepped so many marks that he had long ago forgotten where lines should be drawn. Bolan had lines in the sand the like of which Grozny would not even realize he was trampling over.

"You were wrong," Bolan said simply. There was not the time to explain, and he doubted Grozny would even understand. He was spared the need to elaborate when his cell went off.

"Mr. Cooper, it's Clelland…" The young man's voice was strong this time, alert and clear. "I called in a few favors and reminded people why they owe me. The order of the day has been passed along, and the ground staff at court are aware that it isn't the Koninklijke who will be handling this transfer. They know it will be a private vehicle, though they don't know the make. They have ID for the prisoner and will eyeball him. I can't vouch for what they do then, but if they're straight, then they will be ready for you."

"Thanks, Gordon, that's all I needed to know. It's better if they don't have a vehicle ID at this stage. If I need you again—"

"I carry this cell at all times, Mr. Cooper. I'd wish you luck, but I figure you rely on more than that."

After the line went dead, Bolan mused that Brognola had struck lucky with Gordon Clelland. A few more like him, and like Jack Grimaldi, and this wouldn't be such a skin-of-the-teeth operation.

Speaking of which, time was pressing and he knew that Grimaldi would have the Saab in place.

"Time to go," he said simply.

They left the apartment with Bolan at point. It was early

morning, and there were few signs of life on the block, just the odd shift worker and some mothers dropping their children off at school before heading off to work themselves.

Just as the Executioner was heading off to work.

Bolan was sure that they had not been followed or scoped out in the past couple of days, but still he was alert and on edge as they made their way down to the street, the Micro-Uzi concealed but still to hand. Oddly, the thought that Grozny may try to make a run for it did not cross his mind—the warlord had made it clear by his actions that he did not trust those who sought to release him, and to try to run would play into their hands with nothing in his locker for backup. Despite his complaints, his only hope of staying alive was to go to trial.

Bolan led the warlord along the street to where they had left their previous vehicle a couple of nights prior. Presently, standing in the same spot, was the Saab that Grimaldi had promised. Moving to the rear of the vehicle, he groped for the keys under the rear fender. They were taped there as promised, and he ripped them off before hitting the central locking.

Grozny slid into the passenger seat, and as Bolan settled behind the wheel, the warlord said, "You can trust me with a gun. If I shoot anyone in the head, it won't be you. I might even be useful."

Bolan hesitated for a moment—in a sense it went against the grain, but he knew in his gut that Grozny was being truthful. He slipped the Benelli from the duffel bag and handed it to Grozny, who laid it across his lap and covered it with his jacket.

"I feel a little more confident now. Not just in myself, but because you can concentrate on getting us there in one piece."

"Thanks for the vote of confidence," Bolan said as he hit the ignition and pulled out onto the deserted road.

As they neared the center of Den Haag, moving into the narrower streets of the older sections of the city, the traffic began to build up as they ran into the bulk of the morning rush hour. They slowed to a crawl through necessity. Bolan concentrated on the road: in his mind, the schematics of the roadways that he had memorized ran rampant as he tried to figure out a clearer route. He could see Grozny scoping the street, and trusted that task to the older man.

But Bolan was still on the alert, and noted with interest as they crossed a junction where the traffic signals appeared to be controlled by a workman at the signal's junction box. From the blaring of angry drivers, he figured that the signals had been running erratically, and this may account for some of the snarl up.

He wasn't surprised to note that the workman looked more than a little anxious—as if something more important than fixing traffic lights was on his mind.

It was beginning.

8

The Serb at the junction box didn't notice the Saab in among all the cars that passed him. He wouldn't even have known what type of car the target would be using to approach the court building. What he did know was that he and the two other guerrillas who had been assigned to snarl up the traffic signals were to stick to a strict schedule. So it was because of that he had a closer eye on his watch than he had on the flow on the road before him.

"Time minus five," he heard in his earpiece. The hands-free mic dangled around his throat. He grunted in reply, and then looked up.

The Saab was out of his eyeline.

"WHAT KIND OF VEHICLE are we supposed to be looking out for?" the gate guard asked as he surveyed his inventory for the day and passed the first vehicle on the list through the barriers leading to the court entrance. "I just have a time and a blank space. No license, no make, no nothing. Any bastard could claim to be him."

"Relax," Yvgeny Ushenko murmured as he looked over the other's shoulder at the listing. "He'll have Grozny. You know what that fucker looks like, right?"

The gate guard shrugged. "He's been here before… I watch TV, right?"

"Then there is your answer," Ushenko said with a shrug. "Now, chill and just do the job. Don't worry—what can happen?"

"I suppose… Hey," the gate guard added as Ushenko walked away, cradling his H&K MP-5, "I thought you weren't on until next Tuesday?"

"Had to switch shifts with Florian," Ushenko called back. "You know how he is, him and his stomach."

"He'd better watch his sick leave, or else they'll start a disciplinary against him," the gate guard said sagely.

"That's right," Ushenko returned, adding in quieter tones, "and that's what he'll get after today."

"YOU IN PLACE?" the heavyset Serb muttered into his headset as he hurried from his unmarked truck across to the building directly opposite the courthouse. He weaved through the slow-moving traffic, drivers registering their frustration with blasts that drowned engine noise. He carried a box that looked just like any maintenance man's tool chest. The average maintenance man, picking it up by mistake, would baulk at what it held.

"I'm round the back, entrance in view," crackled back at him. "I'm in position. Radjan is, too. I can see him from here," the voice said with a chuckle.

The young guerrilla was adopting the disguise of a roofer working on the court. Scheduled works were taking place, and it took only the right amount of cash to exchange ID cards and passes with a homesick Polish worker who could return home sooner than he had expected.

"Good, good," the Serb leader murmured. "I will be in position myself in two minutes. Commencement in one."

"Grozny is not here yet, for Chrissake's," his compatriot snapped.

"Don't worry. Blacksuit will deliver on time, and what's about to happen will only shoot a rocket up his ass."

"STUPID TRAFFIC. WHY don't these bastards move quicker?" Grozny complained, slapping the dash of the car hard with his hand.

Bolan ignored the outburst, guiding the car through the crawling traffic—something very odd was happening to the flow this morning, which was just as he would expect. The only thing he could do was to keep sharp and try to find a way through to the court—he was due in a few minutes, and was keen to keep to time as this was the only indicator of identity he would initially have.

He swung the car round a corner, sliding into a gap between a truck and a 4x4. The court building was in sight. It would be quicker if they could get out and walk, but at least while they were in a vehicle they had some degree of anonymity.

"You don't want to speak to me now, Cooper? You won't even answer, or even drive on the fucking sidewalk?"

"Don't take your anger out on me," Bolan replied quietly. "I'm not going to drive on the sidewalk without cause and draw attention to us. And look at it this way—if we're moving slow, you can bet your ass that the enemy is, too."

"It is my ass you're betting," Grozny said with a growl.

"Fair point." Bolan shrugged.

It was then that they heard the explosion.

THE SERB JAMMED the signal box, putting the lights in that area on a permanent red and gridlocking traffic for half a mile. He knew that at that moment his two colleagues were doing the same thing. A half-mile radius around the courthouse was successfully rammed and jammed. Nothing could move, and—more important—nothing could get in and out by road.

He grinned slyly. He had to hand it to the fat idiot who had become their leader, it was a smart move to plan a snatch that was followed by an underground getaway, moving beneath the gridlock above. So smart that it must have been someone else's idea.

Putting this thought to one side, he picked up his tool bag and ran between the cars, crossing the road and heading toward the court. He had a job to do along the way, but first he needed to get away from the small Renault van that had brought him to this spot before it blew up.

He was a thousand yards away, one eye on the second hand of his watch, when the stone lintel of a nineteenth-century administrative building loomed before him. Thanking God that things had been built to last and withstand anything back then, he ducked into it. A startled concierge in uniform made to challenge him—this, after all, was not the kind of man to usually use this entrance. Puzzled, he opened his mouth to speak while wondering why the man had flattened himself against the wall before any such thought was driven from his mind, like the air from his lungs, by a deafening explosion that shattered the glass door and all the windows surrounding him.

It was echoed within seconds by two more explosions as the other two Renault vans used by the fake signalmen also went off.

The Serb took a BXP-10 from the bag, stuffing into his pockets some spare ammunition before hoisting the bag and its other ordnance onto his shoulders like a backpack. Sucking in a deep breath and steeling himself as he had preceding every combat nearly twenty years before, he stepped out of the doorway and began to run at a jog toward the court building, knowing that his two compatriots would be doing the same thing.

As he ran, he heard a short burst of gunfire from a couple blocks away. Something he was compelled to copy as an armed policeman, in the middle of quelling a rising panic among startled motorists and pedestrians, stepped away from the pack and toward him, hand reaching for his firearm as he framed a question that he would not be able to voice. A short burst from the BXP-10 stitched him across the chest and face, propelling him back into the throng. As the gunman would have expected, those unused to combat panicked at the sight of blood and scattered in confusion, into each other, and across his path. Another tap, indiscriminate, caught one woman in the thigh. She hit the sidewalk screaming, while those around her parted as if the flagstones beneath their feet were the Red Sea.

The Serb ran past the prone woman. He had no wish—nor the time—to finish her off. By parting the crowds, she had served her purpose—while at the same time easing his way toward the court building and the target.

CHAOS FOLLOWED THE BLASTS. A moment of stunned nothing, and then the crowds in and out the vehicles around them erupted. People on the sidewalks rushed away from the sounds of the explosions, running into each other as they came from the triangulation points of the blasts, converging and colliding with those in a central area who had no idea which way to turn. Some drivers attempted to run their vehicles onto the sidewalks to skip past the congestion or try to turn, finding only that they ran into each other or phalanxes of pedestrians, jamming on brakes and blaring warnings that went unheeded.

Bolan cursed under his breath, while Grozny was louder

and more forceful in his curses. The soldier's mind raced. If this was an attack on them, then it made little sense to blow up three points at a distance—unless the triangulation was intended to trap them at this point, where they would be sitting targets. Certainly, as he scanned the chaos beyond the windshield, that would be a workable theory. It could be a diversion, but he doubted that—surely their enemy would know if they had arrived at court. No, the only thing that made sense was to assume that this was to trap them and then take them out.

In which case the last thing they needed was to be sitting here.

"Out," he yelled at Grozny, reaching over and grabbing the duffel bag from the backseat.

"I thought you'd never ask," the warlord grunted as he heaved himself and the Benelli out of the passenger seat and onto the road, dropping the cover so that the gun was in full view. Even in the confusion, there were some who came up short on seeing the shotgun, trying to move back against the tide.

"Which way are we going?" Grozny snapped.

"There—" Bolan indicated the court building before leading off. He looked back to check that the warlord was on his heels. "And don't wave that about. I don't want bystanders shot," he yelled above the confusion, indicating the Benelli.

"Cooper, this is war," Grozny yelled back with a vulpine grin. "Anyone gets in the way takes their chance."

"Not with me. You loose that into the crowd without cause and I'll take you down myself," Bolan shouted. As he spoke, he scanned the area around them for potential enemies. The crowds were dense and confusing in their movements, making it hard to recce for threats. They could come out of anywhere, and he was damn sure that the Serbs would have no compunction in taking out anyone innocent who was in the line of fire.

Even as this raced through his mind he was making a path through the throng of people. The Micro-Uzi in his fist was a good machete substitute, cutting through the crowds like a blade through foliage. He could almost feel Grozny's breath on the back of his neck; he could for sure hear it coming hard as the warlord struggled to keep up.

Bolan slowed his pace, turning to let the aging fighter keep up, and that's when he saw a rat-faced, whip-thin man in overalls cutting a path toward them. The man was able to move so swiftly because he had the same advantage as Bolan and Grozny—the BXP-10 he held at midriff level. From the glittering expression in his eyes, even at such a distance, there was no doubt that he had just the one thing on his mind.

Grozny was likely to be safe from fire—they would want to take him alive at this point. No, it was Bolan who would be the target, and the only reason he wasn't already roadkill was because Grozny stood in the line of fire.

In the line of fire—and presently facing the onrushing gunman. Bolan heard him rack the Benelli, and knew that at this range it would rip the gunman to shreds, but also take out a number of innocent citizens.

"No!" Bolan exclaimed, grabbing Grozny's arm with his left hand and forcing the shotgun down before the warlord could pressure the trigger. At the same time he lifted the Micro-Uzi and tensed the muscles in his right arm. Hit the target and not those around—it was an imperative.

Blotting out the noise and chaos around him, ignoring the pull of Grozny as the warlord struggled to loose the grip, the only thing he saw was the Serb coming toward him. He could see the man tense as he made to tighten his trigger finger.

Not if he could help it, Bolan thought as he flexed and tapped a short burst that stitched the man across the chest and abdomen.

The soldier knew it was a good hit, and before the Serb had even hit the sidewalk he was pulling Grozny after him. There was no time to make sure it was a kill; enough to know that the man was down and that they could gain ground.

"Good shot," the warlord said as he struggled to keep up with Bolan while they carved their way through the crowds.

"Save your breath—unless you spot another enemy," Bolan said. The court was in sight. There were guards clustered around the public entrance and the barrier leading to what he would call the tradesman's entrance. They were expecting a car, not two men on foot with guns. The automatic response would be to fire first and ask second. That was assuming that they were all honest, and there were no plants who could take advantage of such an opportunity.

All the while, Bolan kept an eye for both enemy gunmen and for local law enforcement: he hoped that they wouldn't run into any, as there would be no chance to explain and the last thing he wanted was to have to take down an innocent body.

Of course, it was inevitable that both things would occur at once.

As they reached the last junction before the court building, the crowds seemed to part as though offering them a clear path—it was too good to be true.

It became apparent almost immediately that the reason for their parting was the onrush, from two directions, of an armed policeman who was charging toward the direction of one blast and the oncoming Serb gunman, brandishing his BXP-10, who was responsible for the blast.

Bolan could see them rushing toward each other, and

hear Grozny's low chuckle as he, like Bolan, realized that they were caught in the middle of the two.

The policeman slowed, catching sight of what appeared to be three armed men coming from two directions. He was hesitant, unsure of whether he should aim for the duo first, or try to take out the lone gunman.

The Serb had no such doubts: his view was focused solely on Bolan and Grozny. It made up the soldier's mind. As the police officer yelled something in Dutch, but in an incomprehensible, garbled manner, Bolan swung round to face the Serb.

The two men fired almost simultaneously, Bolan's tap running straight and true, pitching the Serb forward as it hit so that his fire was deflected. How tight it had been between the two men was born testament by the chips of paving slab that plucked at Bolan's legs.

No time to worry about what might have been—the Serb was out of the game, and Bolan turned to the policeman, who was frozen, mouth agape, and confused by what he had just seen. Obviously he had expected them to band together against him. As if this were not enough, Grozny was holding his hands aloft, the Benelli dangling in one fist, in a gesture of supplication.

"C'mon, he won't bother us," Bolan said as he grabbed the warlord and pulled him in train toward the court building, leaving the policeman still wondering what exactly was going down.

That was his problem—Bolan's was simple math. Three explosions, two men down following—there was at least one man still in the crowds, and they had a hundred yards to cover. The guards ringing the entrances were trying to marshal the crowd, some of whom were looking for sanctuary in the court building. Overhead, he could hear the sound of choppers in the distance, rapidly approaching.

Of course, it was the only way to get law enforcement into the area, given the gridlock. Would they be Koninklijke or army? He'd feel better if he had to deal with the army, given his prior experience with the paramilitary-police arm.

He'd feel best of all if he could get through the crowd and into the court with Grozny, both of them still in one piece.

The entrance he had planned to use was flush to pavement level and was surrounded by clamoring crowds, some of whom sought entry and others the reasons that the armed guards were not coming to their aid, merely standing there. It was an angry and confused mob, and there was no way he could bust through easily without risking fire from unsighted guards.

The public entrance, on the other hand, was raised enough for the guards standing before it to get a view of the crowds in front of them. They could get a better view of who approached, and who parted the crowds—which was exactly what the sight of two armed men was doing.

Two of the guards yelled at Bolan in guttural Dutch accents. He picked out something about dropping the weapons, but before he and the warlord were forced to yield the only defense they had against a hidden enemy in the crowd, he heard another of the guards exclaim, and caught Grozny's name in the middle of the tangled sentence.

Bolan heaved a sigh of relief—as he had hoped, the warlord had been recognized, and it seemed that at least one guard was aware of who they should have been expecting.

This realization galvanized the guards at the entrance, and they moved down into the crowd, parting those who had not yet been moved away by the sight of the armed men at their rear. They formed a phalanx that allowed Bolan and Grozny to enter the building.

Inside, the marble hallway was quiet: most of the security personnel had focused on protecting the outside, and there were only a few legal personnel milling about, casting curious glances at the two armed men.

Bolan breathed a sigh of relief. The first part of the morning's mission had been achieved. Grozny was in the building. Next he just had to make sure that the trial began with the defendant still alive.

9

The heavyset Serb watched from across the concourse as the man in the blacksuit and Grozny engaged in conversation with two men, one in uniform and one in a suit. He could not hear what they said as he wore a headset that blotted out much of the ambient sound in the hall. But it did keep him in touch with his people, and as long as he had the two men in visual contact, what they said didn't matter.

The headset was disguised by his cover—telecoms engineer working on the fiber optics fed through a wall channel. It was the perfect cover to cut off the court from the outside world when they began their assault. He knew from the sparse communication that he was two men down—no doubt, he thought, the work of the man in the blacksuit.

There was still one man on the outside, one on the roof and four others beside himself on the inside. Added to this, there were three guards that he knew were paid to ease their path. Their ID photos had been sent to him the evening before so that his cell could familiarize themselves with these paid allies.

He regretted the loss of his men, but the bigger picture dictated that they carry on. The aim was still the same. He checked his watch. They were within the limits that had been set. He knew that choppers were on the way in. Air and road would be blocked or covered. It would take at least fifteen minutes for the aircraft to land and discharge their forces. By that time, he and his men would be long gone.

The man in the blacksuit probably thought he was home free—they would soon make him think again.

BOLAN WAS FRUSTRATED and angry, and it was all he could do to keep his temper in check. The commander of the court guard was either obtuse or was one of those who had been paid off. He kept insisting that Grozny would be safe in the holding cell and that Bolan should be debriefed. This despite the soldier's continued insistence that there was as much of a threat within the court as on the outside.

The fool of a commander laughed this off, claiming that they were locked down, and that the crowds on the outside would soon be controlled and any threat mopped up. He even stooped to patronizing Bolan by pointing out with heavy sarcasm that his own actions had contributed to the chaos.

The legal administrator was not much help, either— he backed up the guard commander on keeping Grozny in the holding cells until the army had cleaned up the area.

"You don't get it, do you?" Bolan said slowly, his rage almost boiling over. "I have information that an attack could also be mounted from inside the building. Given that their aim is to stop the trial and take the prisoner, if we get him in court and begin proceedings, then half of their aim has been eradicated. And it will be easier to defend a courtroom than a cell that could be guarded by an enemy."

"I cannot put the judges and counsel at such a risk," the administrator said, shaking his head.

"As long as this man is here and the trial hasn't commenced, everyone in the building is at risk," Bolan said coldly.

"I just cannot take your paranoia seriously." The guard

commander spoke in a dismissive and derisory tone. "You shoot your way in here causing God knows how much damage, then accuse me of having men on the take. And now you are saying that unless we put more people at risk, then there will be another attack? This is the problem with you Americans. You see enemies at every turn and shoot accordingly. It is no wonder that you are so disliked."

Bolan couldn't decide if the man was just being insulting, or if he really was as stupid as he seemed.

"Look," the soldier said in a forceful tone, "I've just come through three explosions and a planned gridlocking of traffic to try to stop us from getting here. I have intel about the bribery of guards to enable access to the court building. The fact that most of your men are being forced to defend the entrances to the building must tell you something."

The guard commander shrugged. "It tells me that there is trouble outside and civil panic, and this is something that is being met with contingency plans by our national forces. It does not confirm anything else that you have said. Which, frankly, seems like nothing more than paranoia that..."

The commander tailed off, angry and bemused by the fact that Bolan was no longer listening to him—he was, in fact, more concerned with a maintenance man down the hall. The guard commander was about to say something more when circumstance cut him off for good.

From the roof of the building came a crack and a muffled explosion. Bolan recognized it as Semtex rather than a grenade or rocket. They must have someone up there, Bolan figured—in which case why not inside? He had already been distracted by the way the maintenance man messing with the fiber optics seemed to be a little too concerned with his job at a time when everyone else was distracted by what had been happening in the streets.

Bolan's instinct was proved right when the explosion above them was matched by a threat from this direction—the maintenance man pulled a BXP-10 from the tool bag at his feet, and in a crouch loosed a burst of fire where Bolan was standing with the warlord and the two officials.

He hit the deck, using his free hand to push the man closest to him—the guard commander. Openmouthed and about to launch into a diatribe about the soldier's paranoia, he had only a second or two to reconsider his position before a wild shot from the Serb's ill-directed burst split his head. The legal administrator stood, frozen in fear: it was only by dint of the Serb's poor marksmanship that he remained alive. Bolan would have flattened him, too, if he had been able. He could only hope that the poor shooting would help the man's luck hold as he took aim with his own Micro-Uzi.

A deafening roar from behind him stayed his hand. It was probably only his imagination, but Bolan was sure that he could feel the heat of the Benelli's load as it discharged over his head. Grozny was quicker off the mark, maybe because he hadn't bothered to aid anyone as he dropped to one knee; maybe because fear was sharpening his long-dulled combat instinct.

There was nothing wrong with his aim. Even though the spread of the shot from the Benelli gave him a greater scope for wild shooting, nonetheless, the bulk of the pellets hit home on their intended target, taking the Serb out of the action permanently.

"Come on, Cooper, we don't have time to hang around here. This is fucked," the warlord screamed, half tapping and half pulling at Bolan as he passed him, already at a run. Bolan had no idea where Grozny thought he was going, but in one thing he was right: there was no way that the trial would start on this day. And with an attack from above and men inside—possibly some in uniform—this was not a secured site.

Bolan was on his feet and level with the warlord before they had passed the slick of blood spreading around the dead Serb. In his head the big American was running through the schematics of the building that he had downloaded and studied the night before. There were escape routes to the rear of the building and the exits used for fire and also for the reception of prisoners. But these were bound to be heavily guarded both as possible points of escape and also as points of entry for those guards still expecting an attack from outside.

No need for that—the enemy was already within. The problem was simply this—how many of those men in uniform understood this, and how many of them were presently the enemy?

Grozny hit the stairwell and started to ascend.

"Where the hell do you think you're going?" Bolan snapped.

"Roof. You get your man with the fucking big chopper in here, and now," Grozny yelled at him.

"No—they'll be coming down this way. We need to find another way out."

"Where? There isn't one," Grozny roared.

Bolan had no time for explanations, and fortunately he was spared the need by the appearance of two Serbs in working man's clothes clattering down the stairwell and into view with BXP-10s raised. Grozny was facing away from them: he would have no time to turn, and his back presented an easy target should they decide that to just take him out was a reasonable option at this point.

Bolan swore loudly as he hit the men with a sustained

burst of fire from the Micro-Uzi, stitching both of them across the torso and causing them to fall down the remainder of the stairs. With no time to worry, he hit them with two more short bursts that ensured they would not get up and fight.

"Come on," he yelled, grabbing the warlord and pulling him in train.

They hit the main corridor again. Guards charged past them, headed for the upper levels where the assault from the roof was still a priority. Bolan indicated that they head back toward the area where they had taken out the Serb leader. Grozny made to question him, but the pace that the soldier set did not allow him time nor breath to frame the question.

As Bolan ran, he mentally scanned the schematics of the building. He had no idea that the guerrillas had also been thinking on these lines. His focus was on getting Grozny out of the building and the immediate area as soon as possible. Then he would need Grimaldi's backup.

They came to an access stair leading to the building's basement. Bolan shoved Grozny through the door, turning to cover their backs and see if they were being followed; then he proceeded in the warlord's wake.

"Where the hell—" Grozny began.

"Save your breath," Bolan snapped. He could have cursed again—anyone may expect footsteps on the stairs, but the warlord had just given himself away with his need to talk.

Bolan's apprehension was proved right as a uniformed guard appeared at the bottom of the stairs.

"Hey, it's okay—" Grozny began, but was cut short as the guard raised his SMG. In this confined space he would not have to shoot with any accuracy for collateral damage.

Bolan pushed the warlord down the stairs before him—the old man might get a few bruises, but that was preferable to what was awaiting him if he stayed upright. Before Grozny even had a chance to swear, Bolan had tapped the Micro-Uzi, stitching the guard across the chest. As the man pitched forward he continued with another burst, and the flight of the guard took his head into the path of the shot, finishing the job.

Bolan flinched as the guard's almost instinctive tap went awry, the shot ricocheting off the walls and the metal of the stairwell. Bolan could do nothing except hope that his luck held.

"—fuck is going on," Grozny yelled angrily as he pulled himself up onto his feet, the first part of his imprecation lost in the whine and clatter of the firefight.

"Inside men. They've paid off guards as well as getting in themselves. So we've got to get out."

"But how—"

"Shut up and follow me," Bolan ordered, in no mood—and with no time—to explain.

On this level, there was access to a service tunnel that was used partly as an emergency exit and entrance to ferry men into the building, and partly for maintenance of the plant that kept the building functioning. It would lead them into a network that connected all the international court buildings in this section of the Hague. Bolan's concern was that there may be others down here—enemy or misguided ally—that would fire on sight.

Along the way there was another access tunnel that would allow them to enter the sewer system. According to the plans he had in his head, it was a secured door. Bolan was still carrying some ordnance that would take care of that.

But first they had to make the distance. The tunnel was

lit by low-level strips, with shadows lurking at the turns that could harbor a threat. Their footsteps echoed as they made time in a jog-trot, both men keeping their weapons pointed downward, but with hearts pounding from more than just exertion.

They were within five hundred yards of the access door Bolan sought when fate intervened. Their own footsteps masked any that approached, and the same could be said for anyone approaching from the opposite direction. So it was that they reached a bend in the tunnel and were suddenly faced with two men—one a uniformed court guard, the other a Serb in workman's clothes—who had crested a turn coming from the opposite direction.

Bolan immediately tapped twice, hitting the two men. The guard was hit in a line across the torso and went down never to rise again. But the Serb was quicker than the guard, and although the burst caught him in the leg, the fact that he was the second in Bolan's line of fire gave him that fraction of a second he needed to dodge the main burst.

As he fell, he hit them with a burst from his BXP-10. The line of fire was wide and high, but one ricochet hit Grozny in the arm, causing him to curse loudly as he fell to one knee. Bolan ignored this—there would be time enough for the warlord once he had eliminated the threat. He took a step forward and tapped once more. Before the Serb had a chance to return any fire, the shot from the Micro-Uzi ended his resistance.

Bolan turned to Grozny. "Can you move?"

"It's only my arm," he hissed. "I'm not that old and fucked yet."

Bolan was pleased to hear the old bastard being so ornery. He'd need that to get them through the rest of the escape route. Moving ahead as Grozny stumbled in his wake, Bolan made the five hundred yards to the secured door.

The lock was strong, but not as strong as a small clump of C-4 with a detonator timed for thirty seconds. He primed the detonator and then moved back, holding up an arm to halt the warlord. They took what cover they could in the tunnel as the explosive decimated the lock and part of the metal of the service door, swinging it open and revealing the ladder leading down to the main sewer.

"Down," Bolan snapped.

Grozny took the ladder slowly, wincing as he put weight on the damaged arm. The Benelli was slung over his shoulder, and the injury slowed him up and made him vulnerable—the last thing Bolan wanted.

While Grozny descended, Bolan kept watch. The tunnel was empty and there was no sound other than the cursing of the warlord and the splashing of his last steps down into the sewer. Satisfied that they had eliminated the only threat, Bolan followed the warlord down the ladder, slinging the Micro-Uzi over his shoulder until he hit the watery depths.

"You leave the door?" Grozny questioned. "What if they follow?"

"By the time any of them left standing get this far, we'll be well away from here. We haven't got the time to waste," Bolan answered.

He struck out to the east. According to the schematic that was hot-wired into his brain at this moment, if they took this route and bore left at the next junction, they would come up outside the area delineated by the triangular traffic blasts.

Once they were out, the real fight would begin. He would need Grimaldi to find a safe house, and then he would need to pin down the source of funding for the Serb group. After this action, he was almost certain that the guts had been ripped from the group. But as long as the source of their funding remained there was a threat, both from the remnants of the group and from those who paid them—and would pay others.

The only way to eradicate that threat was to cleanse it with fire.

10

"I am getting old. Useless…" Grozny was feeling sorry for himself as he flexed the wounded arm that Bolan had just dressed. He grimaced at the pain and at his own perceived weakness. "There was a time when I would have thought nothing of such a wound. I would keep on as though it was not there. But today…today I felt it drag me down, slow me. I could not have made it back if I was on my own. And that hurts. Hurts more than this scratch ever could," he continued, gesturing to his wounded arm with his uninjured hand. "Maybe they should just lock me away, you know? Maybe that is all I am good for now."

Bolan had no time for Grozny's self-pity as he packed the med kit. "Listen, what we both need to focus on now is wiping out this threat. Otherwise, I'm not going to get back to Washington and you're not even going to get the chance to feel sorry for yourself in prison."

Grozny managed a wry grin. "True."

"It's still locked down and a mess out there, so we need to hole up for a while," Bolan said.

"And then?"

"And then you sit tight and wait. I've got some work to do."

Grozny assented. "This is your fight now. I have to concede."

Bolan was bemused. Though it was a compliment from a man from whom he did not welcome such an accolade, Bolan also knew that coming from Grozny, it was one hell of a concession.

"You can fix us some rations. I need to catch up with what's happening. I'll brief you when I have full intel."

Grozny looked the soldier full in the face before nodding briefly. "I appreciate. You have no imperative to do this."

As the warlord left the room, Bolan paused in thought. This was a side of the warlord that he had not seen, and it made him understand some of the qualities that had made him a charismatic leader—though evil nonetheless. But this was not the moment for contemplation—there were pressing matters at hand.

His first call was to Grimaldi.

"Sarge, you made it okay?"

"I'm here, Jack, and not dead in a sewer."

"You should have got me to fly you in and out. I could have taken care of that asshole on the roof, and there would have been no need to deal with those blasts at ground level."

"They would have gone off, anyway, Jack. The idea was to keep it low-key."

"Sarge, there has been nothing low-key about this from the beginning. These guys have about as much security sense as a five-year-old. The only way we should have tackled this was to take Grozny into our care from the beginning. Then blast the hell out of these terrorists before they could do too much damage."

Bolan laughed. "Diplomacy was never your strong point, Jack—"

"Or yours, Sarge. Action when it's called for. Plus, I'm tired of being an errand boy on the end of a phone."

"I know. But you've kept us alive with the safe houses. And I couldn't call you in when we were moving out of the court. There was no way we could stay aboveground. Listen, I'm going on the offensive with these guys. I'm going to need you to back me up like you know best."

"Sounds good to me. I'll prep and await your call."

"Good man. Wait for me, Jack. I've got to tackle Hal first, and he's not going to like this."

Bolan wasn't far wrong in his assumption. Brognola was not pleased to hear the details of Bolan's report, but he knew that the soldier was doing the best he could under the current circumstances. And he also knew he was lucky to have Bolan on the ground handling the situation—the mission would have been lost long ago otherwise.

"Hal, there's only one way we can bring resolution here. Grozny wants to stand trial. We want him to. According to you, some elements in the Chinese regime don't. Neither do the terrorist cell they're funding. Most of those guys must be dead by now. If we're going to get through this, I need to keep Grozny safe here, and take out the remaining terrorists. And then…"

"I don't know, Striker. That could cause an international incident—"

"I know, Hal," Bolan interrupted. "But politics isn't my job. But I *can* do my job, and satisfy any questions you might get, if I have the right information. It's not all the Chinese. They've got one man here who is behind this, if Clelland is right. Eliminate him, and they'll want to keep it quiet, for whatever their reasons. Once Grozny has gone into the dock, it's all over. All I have to do is knock him out without getting caught or causing too many fireworks."

Brognola sighed. "This has been nothing but fireworks so far…. But if it's the only way…"

"Hal…can you suggest any other course to bring this down quickly?"

There was a moment's silence.

"Dammit, I can't…"

"Then let me play it my way. If it all goes belly-up, then you can deny responsibility."

"No. That's not what this is about. Besides, your intel will be coming through me."

"It doesn't have to. Leave it with me, log this call as you must and then leave me to go rogue. Just for a day or two."

"I don't like it, Striker."

"Hal, I'm not giving you the choice," Bolan said sharply, disconnecting the call. From here on out communication with the big Fed and with Stony Man Farm must cease until he had tidied up matters at this end.

He turned to find that Grozny standing in the doorway.

"Food is ready," he said simply, turning away. Bolan followed him to the kitchen of the safe house. They were in an apartment that, bizarrely, was in a concierged block. Grimaldi had played a double bluff with this location—they were in a relatively prosperous section, near the northeast suburbs and on the edge of the old city. The concierge had been paid off from the war chest that Bolan had made available to Grimaldi, with the ace pilot murmuring something about gambling debts and a sister he had "gotten out of some trouble" when asked how the concierge's loyalty could be guaranteed. And though the apartment did not appear to be secured from the outside, the interior had been fitted out by the flier with tech that would tell them if a fly so much as coughed within a hundred yards of any ingress. Added to which, surveillance fiber optics CCTV'd the immediate area and the stairwell, elevator and reception area of the building.

They ate in silence. Grozny was a decent scratch field cook, and after the day they had endured Bolan was still a little surprised at how hungry he was when it came to it. As they ate, he noticed that the warlord was eyeing him.

He said nothing. It was only when they had finished that Grozny broke the silence.

"So you have a plan? I was listening, I admit. This is too small an apartment to pretend not to."

Bolan nodded. "I need to gather some more intel, but it's pretty obvious what I have to do—and that I need to take myself off the map so that there can be no questions asked."

"How much time do you have?"

"The sooner I get it done the better. I figure that you won't be able to leave here for a few days as it'll take at least that long to get the court in a good enough condition to resume. That or arrange another venue. Either way, you need to stay here."

"You trust me on my own?"

Bolan grinned. "I don't think I have a choice. Though I don't think you have many options left open, and I take you to be a realist. But your reactions would be slow with the injury. You need a babysitter."

"Shit," Grozny grumbled. "I hate the fact that I can only agree with you on this."

"Don't sweat it. I think you'll like your babysitter," Bolan said, wondering how Grimaldi would take the assignment when he was told.

But before this, he had to garner more information. There was only one man who could help him. His cell was taking one hell of a battering, and Bolan hoped that the line was still secured. He would have to trust Kurtzman's skills.

"Mr. Cooper. You had one hell of a day today, sir. Good to hear that you're in one piece. And our friend, I trust?"

"He is. And he'll stay that way. I have someone who can help me with that. How long do we need to keep him secured?"

"Two days. This has caused one hell of a stink. About

damn time, if you ask me—security in this city needed a shake-up. Shame it took this. Good thing is that the agencies who've been trying to score points rather than cooperate have realized where that shit has got them, and are pulling together, at least for now. It'll take forty-eight to clean up enough to recommence. The onus is on presenting a front to the world that terrorism cannot stop justice."

"Good. So we keep our man in lockdown for forty-eight, and then get him to court. Meantime, I need to clean up—Eastern Europe and the East, if you know what I'm saying?"

There was a moment's silence, then: "I understand. Mr. Brognola has sanctioned this?"

"No. I need your help, but if you feel—"

"No, sir, I just need to know if this is on or off the record. One of the guards who turned against his own men was taken alive. Debriefing was a little—uh—*brutal* might be the right word. But he gave up some intel about the Serbians who paid off the guards. Time, place, cost. More than that, the level of trust between these assholes is so low that it's heartening in its results. They followed the Serbs, just as insurance. Paid off, I guess, as it'll knock some time off his sentence. So we have a location for where the remaining cell members live."

"How much time before a raid is mounted?"

"It'll be twenty-four. The agencies are working together, but in some ways that slows them up. It gives you time as a mobile unit to get in first."

"Exactly my thoughts," Bolan affirmed. "And after them, the East."

There was a pause. When Clelland spoke again, his tone was hesitant. "I have details on the man who liaised with the Serbs. Research suggests that he was familiar with your boy two decades back. Maybe ask him about that. As for where he is now, I can furnish as much as I can gather, but it's the Chinese embassy, man. No one who isn't Chinese knows much about what goes on behind those walls."

"Give me everything you have, about both locations. I'll do the rest. The least you know…"

"I understand," Clelland agreed. "I'll send you all my intel. Just give me a half hour to make a few calls, Mr. Cooper."

"I appreciate that. From this moment, you know nothing and you've never heard of me. If necessary…but I hope that won't be the case," Bolan added.

While he was waiting for the intel, he figured, it was time to ask Grozny a few questions about his past. Something Bolan had been avoiding up until this point.

The warlord had settled himself in to flick through the news channels. His favorite hobby had an added piquancy as he was the main story on many of them. He looked up as Bolan entered the room.

"They don't know what to make of this." He laughed. "I'm either dead, in captivity or have been kidnapped. Official sources—and we all know what a pile of shit that is—have been quiet. Think they're trying to figure out what to say?"

Bolan did not reply. He took the remote from Grozny and killed the TV.

"I have to ask you something. About the old days."

Grozny's face hardened. "Now you want to talk about it? I didn't notice that before, when I wanted to."

"Things change. Besides, it's not the so-called glory of war that I want to discuss. It's the men who paid for it."

"Man. There was just the one who was my link. He's the one you want to know about?" The warlord's tone was resigned. Bolan assented, and Grozny continued. "They were very careful to keep a low profile. I know I wasn't the only one they were paying. And I know that they had the same method with each approach. One man would handle everything. That way it was easier for him to keep out of sight. I mean, when was the last time you saw a Serb, Slav, Bosniak or even a Russian who looked like a Chinese man? Too many of them, and they were going to stand out. He's the man your boy who you were just talking to saw with the fuckwit who tried to 'rescue' me?"

"I think so. It would make sense if they sent him in to get you out or eliminate you. Who is he?"

"If he's the same one—and I mean *if,* because you'd have to be one hell of a smart bastard to ride the last twenty years in China—then his name is Xiao Li." Grozny studied Bolan's face, and saw the flicker of recognition at the name—just as Bolan wanted. "It makes sense to send him back for me, one way or the other. We didn't spend that long together, I guess. Three years at most. But intense years, Cooper. Years with shit in them that you wouldn't believe…maybe you would. But it's the kind of thing that makes you feel like you've known someone a lifetime. He knows exactly what I'd do and how I'd feel, and I figure that I would have the same knowledge about him."

"He's at the embassy. I need to go after him. Should I kill him or should I send him back with a message? My directive is to avoid an international incident, or at least more of an incident than we have right now. Do I tell him that we are aware of Chinese culpability and that you will say nothing about it in court in return for cessation of activity? It will remain something that will not be made public but will remain between you, those in the Chinese regime who have something to hide and the U.S. government."

Grozny pondered this for a moment. He looked to be deep in thought, his mind dragged back over those years to when he stood side by side with Xiao Li. Finally, and with finality, he spoke.

"You kill him. He goes back with such a message, he will not be allowed to live, anyway, but I think you know that. And he would not deliver such a message, anyway. He would carry on with his mission until he was either captured by the Dutch authorities or killed in the process. And he knows that diplomatic immunity is a death sentence. He has…had…a streak of disdain about him. Arrogance, maybe. He thought he was better than any of us, even though he was just as culpable. He would think himself better than any situation you put him in. Age may have ground him down in some ways, as it does for us all. But not in that way.… There is arrogance like iron in him, Cooper. You really have no option."

Bolan nodded slowly. "It was always headed that way. I just needed to find out if it was worth a shot."

"Don't waste your breath. He wouldn't, believe me."

Bolan left the warlord to his wandering through the news channels. But he knew that Grozny's mind was not on the images and sounds in front of him. There was a faraway look about him that spoke of his mind traversing the years, reliving things that perhaps even he would prefer to forget.

The soldier returned to his room to prepare. Grimaldi had supplied ordnance, and from it Bolan needed to collate an armory that would be enough to take out the remaining Serbs, and also allow him to move straight on to the embassy. Grimaldi would arrive by daybreak to babysit the warlord—this much he knew from the messaging between them after his last call—and Bolan would move immediately on Serb headquarters. That attack would soon reach the ears of Xiao Li, and once that happened, time would be at a premium.

If he allowed enough time to travel, to recce and then

to attack, it would leave him little time to come back into the city and take out Xiao. He could use the cover of night, for what little help it would give. He had to use it—by the following day, Xiao would be actioning any contingency plans.

Bolan checked the time. It was still early, but he ached from the day, and he would need to be rested for the exertions to come. He showered, by which time Clelland had been as good as his word and the intel he needed was on his smart phone.

Bolan lay down to rest, the sound of the TV distant. He must rest, but he doubted that Grozny would be able to.

The soldier was glad that he did not have to live in the warlord's head.

11

Milan had to pass the industrial park again. That was the problem with living so close to the site that had been used as a base. The idea that you hide in plain sight by adopting an everyday existence close to the base had served them well in the first instance. These days it seemed only to mock them as they passed it while going about their everyday business. Their cover, as they had liked to think of it, was all they had left.

Milan was an electrician. Mila worked as a waitress. Slobo was a laborer, and had been working legitimately at the international court a month before the trial had been due to commence. That was how they had gotten the plans to the building. And now they were the only three left.

Scheveningen was a strange area in many ways. The beach area attracted the tourist trade, but there was also a poor part, with properties that were cheap to rent and even cheaper to buy if you had the capital. The industrial parks that had been built for the port that lay near were half empty and derelict—this was what had made it so perfect. The Serbs had bought one of the rooming houses that had been built with one eye on the tourist trade, but had been too near the poverty of the permanent residents to attract trade. This made them good places for those transients who needed inexpensive accommodation. In among these people, and the ever-changing tourist tide, it had been easy to buy the house, move everyone in and set up cover jobs that made them look just like another group of migrant workers.

Just three of them left. The others dead. None had survived the onslaught of the man in black. Who the hell was he? A Special Forces operative of some kind, maybe, but of which nation? Not the Dutch, that was for sure. They had seen in battle that the Koninklijke had little love for him.

It no longer mattered now. He had done what he had to—they were out of the game. With only three of them left, there was no way they could mount another attack to try to get Grozny. Why the hell they wanted the burned-out old has-been had always puzzled Milan. The man had meant something once, but as a figurehead for the new state they had hoped to bring into being...? Maybe his name and notoriety would give them something to show the people as a statement of their intent, but otherwise...

Milan sighed as he entered the house. It was the middle of the afternoon, and usually he wasn't back before six. His mind hadn't been on the job, but it had been simple enough. The ring circuits in an old house needed renewal, and a new trip fuse fitted to prevent any overloading causing a blowout. Overloading because it was an old building being refurbished to become a rooming house, just as their own house was supposed to be. Maybe that was what they should do now that they were reduced to just three. Mila had been kept out of the front line not just because she was a woman—she had been kept out of combat because, if he was honest, Milan knew that she was the real brains of the group.

She would know what to do.

When he let himself into the house, it was the oppressive silence that hit him most of all. The distempered walls were decorated with cheap prints, and the furnishings in each room were equally simple yet comfortable. There was a communal room on the ground floor, and a good kitchen. In his head, Milan could see them leaving behind dreams of greater glory and keeping this place as a rooming house. It would pay its way, and they could still keep their work until it made enough. He would ask Mila about this—she would be able to work out if it was viable for them to do this.

But that was a fantasy. He knew it was—but what was the alternative? To accept that all they had worked for was gone? That they were to be hunted both by the Koninklijke, by Interpol, by any damn agency that they had gone up against? More than that—their paymasters. The Chinese would not be pleased that this had not achieved their ends. The money they had paid would have to be recouped and justified if the mission could not be claimed as a success.

That was the dream of the rooming house shattered. That was any peaceful night's sleep for the rest of his life, no matter how short that might be, equally shattered. They could not stay here. But it would be just as impossible to go on the run. Where could they go that the hand of their paymasters, who were not bound by law and able to operate with impunity, could not find and crush them?

Milan felt like a broken man. He looked around the house, still empty until Mila and Slobo returned from work, with a growing sense of despair before sitting in the communal room, staring out of the window as twilight began to fall.

As he waited, desperation moved beyond despair and into anger. If they could not go quietly, then they would go with blood. It was the only way to justify what had so far been spilt.

BOLAN HAD ARRIVED in the area shortly after two o'clock. When he had called Grimaldi and told him of the slight change in plan, the flier was not too pleased. "Back me up as you know best" meant taking to the air with Dragon-slayer again—not acting as nursemaid to a war criminal awaiting trial. He had grumbled every time Bolan had spoken to him—on the phone when he called him over, and face-to-face when Grimaldi arrived and handed the keys of his car over to the soldier.

"There's inventory in the trunk, just in case you didn't have what you wanted here. And there's some surveillance and detection tech, as well. Cameras and monitors, some mics, stuff like that. So you go and have fun chasing down the bad guys while I sit on my ass watching TV with laughing boy."

Bolan could understand Grimaldi's frustration—he was a fighter, not a security guard. And, at first, Bolan had wanted to use the chopper to go in all guns blazing and take out the opposition with the minimum of effort. What had changed his mind? The fact that such an action would alert the Chinese elements who had interests, for a start—a full-on attack would cause ripples that would have Xiao Li on the first plane back to Beijing in a diplomatic bag. Dead or alive. Similarly, Brognola would have a lot to deal with as it was—to make his task harder when there was a quieter way of doing business would be ultimately self-defeating.

The soldier took Grimaldi's Lexus and headed through the center of Den Haag, away from the safe house to the north and down toward the coast and Scheveningen. On the way down he had time to reflect. The number of men he had personally accounted for over the past few days made it doubtful that there were many left in the group. It was doubtful whether it would be necessary to make the grand gesture: hc should be able to mop them up without causing too much mess.

When he reached the area, he was careful to park up

half a mile from the location he had been given. The Lexus stood out in such a poor district, and Bolan didn't want to draw too much attention to himself. He picked a side street that was in an area of mostly deserted houses and shop fronts. It looked to be an area that was ripe for demolition.

Taking a duffel bag with sound and vision surveillance equipment, and a selection of flash and concussion grenades, he also holstered a Glock 23 semiautomatic with a thirteen-round magazine firing 165 grain Speer Gold Dot JHP slugs, which fitted nicely into a fast draw armpit sling. He also sheathed the Benchmade Stryker automatic knife with the four-inch Tanto blade. He intended to travel light and make the minimum of fuss—if he could use the knife more than a firearm, then so much the better.

He pulled a light coat on over his blacksuit, and put the duffel bag into a common backpack. If he had to proceed on foot, then he wanted to be as inconspicuous as possible.

Not that it seemed to matter as he made his way through the streets that were mostly deserted. And even those people who were around were uninterested in the stranger passing through their midst.

It was the same when he reached the location he was searching for—a nondescript rooming house, one of many like it that lined the street. There was a turnoff three houses down on the opposite side of the road, and he took up position there in order to examine his target in more detail.

IT WAS LATER in the afternoon, and Bolan watched the man named Milan arrive. The Serb, seemingly lost in his own thoughts, did not seem to know that he was being observed.

The house had an air of being deserted. There seemed to be no movement within until the Serb arrived, and Bolan left his position to make a recce of the immediate area. It was not satisfactory—the house was in the middle of a terrace, and the yard at the rear backed directly onto the yard of another house, with no alley for access.

Returning to his post, Bolan was in time to observe another man, a little older and heavier, return, followed shortly after by a woman who looked the same age as the first man.

He waited awhile longer, as twilight fell around him and evening drew toward night. There was no one else returning, and any activity in the house must be at the rear, as the front remained in darkness.

So there were three at least—and maybe at most. The numbers were good, although lack of intel about the interior was a drawback.

Time was moving on—he would have to take action. Bolan crossed the road and approached the house to the left of his target. Knocking on the door, he was received by a sour-faced woman in late middle age.

"What do you want?" she snapped.

"A room. For a few nights. I have work in the area."

She laughed, harsh and cracking. "You're one of the few. Well, it's not like we don't have rooms to let. God knows we could do with new tenants. Not as bad as next door—most of them seem to have left and God knows how they'll get by. But that's not my problem. Now, you want a large room or small?"

"What's the difference?" Bolan asked, taking in the information that the target house had been seriously depleted.

The woman shrugged. "A hundred euros a month. And the stairs. You'll want to know that the cheap rooms are at the top of the house."

Bolan sniffed. "Until this job pays me, best to have the cheap room. After that, who knows? You'll expect a month up front, yes?"

The woman nodded, and led him into the interior of the

house. It was drab and dark, with the smell of stale spices hanging in the air. The furnishing was threadbare like the carpet, and the two men he saw as the landlady led him up the stairs were as drab and downbeat as the house.

But none of this mattered as he handed over a month's rent to the woman while she showed him the tiny room he was getting for his money. The bed looked as if it harbored life, while the cupboard and chairs that comprised the remainder of the furniture looked as though they were made of cardboard. It was unimportant—he had no intention of staying long.

He waited for her to leave, moving to the door to listen as she descended the stairs. When he was sure he was alone, he moved over to the window and opened it up, leaning out to take in the surrounding building.

His room was just under the eaves of the house, and there was a gap of three yards between this window and that of the top room in the target house. There were no obvious foot- or handholds between the two, and the stucco plaster on the walls was peeling and flaking, revealing brickwork beneath that had loose mortar, but not enough to fashion holds in the time available.

He would have to go up. Using the sill of the window, he could grasp the eave and pull himself onto the roof. From there, if he was careful on tiling that was probably in as poor repair as the walls, he could be at the corresponding window in the target house within seconds.

He took a long hard look at the surrounding area. The yards were empty along the terrace. There were only a few windows where he could see in. Where shutters and blinds were drawn, he knew he was safe. Those windows that did have a view seemed to be either empty or showed people preoccupied in their own tasks.

With twilight helping to disguise him as little more than

a shadow, he stripped the coat of labels and left it on the bed. He took the duffel bag from the holdall, which he similarly stripped of identifying marks before leaving that with the coat, and climbed out onto the sill.

The eave was wood and rotten in places. But the metal and plastic of the drain and guttering gave him better purchase. He pulled himself up, using that part of the window that jutted out as a precarious foothold to augment the effort of his upper body. Once on the roof, he spread his weight and tentatively felt his way across the tiles. Some were loose, and the roof joists beneath felt spongy and rotten in part. Despite this, his caution enabled him to make rapid progress.

Lowering himself down off the roof and onto the sill of the upper window was the easy part. Getting in might be another matter. He didn't want to break glass and risk raising the alarm. Praying his luck would hold, he took the knife and slid the blade into the gap between frame and hinge. He ran it along the edge, searching for purchase to prise the window open, or a lock that he could try and break. All the while, he was aware of the strain in his thighs and calves as he huddled on the narrow sill.

It was there—a precious inch of purchase to dig in the knife and lever the unlocked window outward. It was delicate, though. Too much effort would risk him toppling back and off the sill, but too little would leave him trapped and the window closed.

With relief, he managed to get the window open enough to sheathe the knife and use his fingers to better prise it open. After what seemed like hours but was in reality less than thirty seconds, he had the window open enough to climb and set both feet on the floor.

He stopped and breathed deeply, listening to the sounds of the house. He was in—next, the real work began.

"WE SHOULD JUST LEAVE. There is nothing left to fight for. I wish there was, but…" Slobo shrugged and spat on the floor of the basement. Here, the group had the PC and printer on which they prepared, printed and mailed their propaganda. A safe in one corner held what remained of the war chest they had been given by their Chinese sponsors. A steel cabinet and trunk housed what remained of their ordnance. The heavy Serb looked around at it all, sadly. "It is over."

Milan grasped him by the shoulders and looked him in the eye. "No! No, it is not, my friend. I thought this, like you. But I was wrong. Listen to me. We have nowhere to hide. The law and military will be up our ass. And if *they* are not, then the Chinese will be. There is only one thing we can do. Our aim was to found a new state. Maybe we won't be able to do that, but we can go out in a blaze of glory and make our message known. We are not alone. Others will follow."

Mila shook her head. She was standing apart from the other two, and her body language spoke of someone seeking to distance herself.

"I do not want to be a martyr—for anyone or anything. I say that we split what is left and go our own ways."

Milan looked at her in astonishment. "How can you? You know I am right. You are the clever one, yes? You know that they will come after us, that they will hunt us down. Why not strike back when we can?"

"You speak for yourself," she said with bitterness. "I will take my chances."

"You will not," Milan yelled, hitting her with a backhand sweep that knocked her across the room.

"Milan, what the fuck do you think you're doing?" Slobo said, restraining the younger man as he tried to get at Mila.

"No one goes against us. No one. We have always stuck together, and we always will."

The woman picked herself up, her head spinning from where she had hit the wall. "You are not a realist, Milan. You never were. Maybe none of us were. One way or another we are marked for death. I will take my chances and see how long I can have before it catches up with me. I am going to take my share of what is left from the money and leave. If you want to stop me, then so be it."

Calmly, she wiped the blood that had gathered from a cut on her temple and went to the safe. Unlocking it, she took out a pile of cash, which she counted before replacing two-thirds in the safe. She turned and faced the two men defiantly.

"Are you going to try to stop me?"

Slobo looked at Milan. The younger man shook his head. The older Serb said simply, "Go. Good luck."

Mila, her innards like jelly, left the basement and went up to the ground level. She was about to ascend the stairs to pack a bag when a hand stayed her.

There should have been no one else in the house. She was about to yell in shock when another hand clamped over her mouth.

BOLAN'S RECCE OF the house had been swift. The rooms showed signs of occupancy, but were presently empty. He could hear nothing as he moved around. But as he worked his way downstairs, it became obvious that the remaining terrorists were on the ground floor or in the basement—if the latter, then they were a sitting target.

He reached the ground floor, and a recce showed this to also be empty. Bolan took some of the surveillance tech from the duffel bag and used a mic to listen through the closed door to what was going on below. He was able to hear the exchange between the terrorists, which confirmed that there were only three remaining. Make that two, as the woman was about to leave. He left the door and stood out of view in the doorway of an interior room. He watched her as she closed the door behind her and walked to the stairs. She had already ascended a few stairs when Bolan stepped across and stopped her.

"Say nothing and you'll be fine. Try to alert them and you'll be dead before the first word can escape. Understand?"

Bolan made certain that there was no mistaking his tone—and her eyes showed enough understanding for him to believe her.

"You meant what you said?" he asked. Mutely, she assented. He continued. "There are two of them down there? And they have armaments?" She assented to each question.

"Okay. I want you to leave. Now. No delays. You have enough cash to get by. You know that it won't be long before they catch up with you, though you might not have to worry about the Chinese." He shook his head at her mute, questioning glance. "What's going to happen to your ex-compatriots is going to happen to their connection. You've opted out. I'll let you take your chance. Next time, I might not be so lenient."

He indicated the door. Obviously puzzled, perhaps not quite believing that she had escaped death, she seemed unwilling to move. But Bolan's stony glance must have persuaded her, as she walked hesitantly to the door, pausing only to look back at him before closing the door behind her.

Two left. Bolan moved back to the basement entrance and listened again.

"Two, three days and they will have that court open again. They do not want to let us win in any way," Milan said bitterly. "We'll see who the winners are. They will have to bring Grozny to trial, and when they do we will be waiting. I will prepare a statement to release before we leave. We will free him or die in the attempt, taking him with us."

Slobo sighed. "You know, when it comes down to it, I don't want to die now. But then I guess I don't want to ever. Who does? But this will be quick, compared to what the military scum or the Chinese bastards will do to us."

"We must prepare. We have to be ready at a moment's notice. No more working-man shit. Cover's blown. We need to prepare all the weapons we have."

BOLAN CURSED AS he heard Milan's words, and the sound of a metal cabinet being opened. The two men fell silent as they set to their task. It seemed absurd that they would do this at this point. They had time—though perhaps too much. Bolan had seen this many times over the years. Men who knew they were about to go into combat, more than likely to die, and were blanking the possibility from their minds with preparation. What drove them was no longer even their cause—it was the need to shut the fear of death from their minds.

They would not have to worry about that for much longer.

He could send down a grenade and make it a quick and simple process, but that would throw up too much sound, attract too much unwelcome attention. Better that he did this as quietly as possible.

The door down to the basement was unlocked, just as the woman had left it. They were not expecting anyone else, even though they knew that they had become targets. Their thinking was unclear, which made them unpredictable. That was a possible danger. Bolan's next move would have to be quick and decisive.

The soldier opened the door, taking care not to make any noise, and set his foot on the first stair. With the thick door presently open, he could hear the two men quite clearly. There was some heavy breathing and the kind of grunting that comes from shifting heavy objects. For a moment he wondered what kind of ordnance they had down there—there was no way he could leave it, and would have to arrange a mop-up of some kind.

But that could wait until after. He could sense the concentration in their silent efforts. He eased his way down the stairs until he came to a bend that would bring him into view. He held back, observing them. There was a young man going through a case of BXP-10s similar to the ones he had witnessed the Serbian group use all the way through this campaign. He wondered if they were loaded—there was a case of magazines next to it, and it would be reasonable to assume that the SMGs were not presently loaded.

Reasonable wasn't good enough—he would assume that at least one had a chambered round. He slipped the Glock from its holster. It was ready to fire.

The second man was closer to the stairs. He was moving a metal chest that was open, and contained mortars, plastics and what looked from their obscured angle like claymore mines. His head was lowered as he bent over the chest, heaving it across the floor. His labored breathing and the grind of the metal chest on the concrete floor had served to mask any noise that the soldier may have made on the stairs.

He should have been the man that Bolan picked off first, but circumstance had other ideas.

Bolan had lifted the Glock when, more by bad luck than any giveaway sight or sound, the younger man looked up. For a moment, Bolan could see the disbelief in his face. The man's reaction, however, was sharp—the soldier had to grant him this. He snatched up one of the BXP-10s and leveled it—confirming Bolan's suspicion that at least one would have chambered shells—his mouth coming open to shout a warning.

He didn't have the chance. A slight shift of Bolan's body weight and inclination of the arm, and the quick tap that had been intended to take out the closer target sufficed to stitch a line across the young man's chest and abdomen that dropped him before his finger had a chance to tighten on the trigger.

As Bolan tried to readjust, he discovered that fear can overcome shock and surprise and lend a strength that the fearful did not realize they possessed. For, as he shifted, he took in that the older man was no longer bent over the chest. Knowing that his life depended on moving without fear or thought, the Serb had shot forward, and was already up the stairs, head down and charging for Bolan. He was unarmed, and knew that his only chance of survival lay in preventing his enemy from firing and stunning him so that the odds were leveled.

A lesser man than Bolan may have been caught out. Certainly, the Serb had closed on him so quickly that he couldn't bring the Glock around to fire on him; but as he wanted to avoid noise, that may not be a bad thing. As the heavy man cannoned into him, Bolan rolled back, riding the impact. He brought his legs up as much as possible, to try to give him some purchase in the other's midriff. At the same time he brought the Glock down on the man's back and neck, using it as a club. Ideally, he would have hit him on the neck and laid him out, but the angle was not the best. The glancing blow did slow the Serb's momentum, however, and allow Bolan to lever him backward with his knees.

The heavy man stumbled on the narrow stairs, wavering before falling back, only panic and the luck of hitting solid stair with his back foot stopping him from going flat on his back.

Not that this would do him much good. As he flailed, Bolan dropped the Glock and launched himself forward. He barreled into the man, driving him back onto the concrete and driving the air from his lungs. While the man flailed for air, Bolan clamped his hands around the Serb's throat, reaching for the carotid and stopping the blood flow.

The flailing ceased as the Serb lost consciousness. Bolan continued his grip until life followed consciousness. He didn't like killing a man this way, but it was quick and it was quiet, and it was clean. He could have used his knife, but he had to walk back to his car—the noise of the short tap on the Glock was bad enough, but to leave a blood trail and to be marked would be unforgivable.

Sure that both men were permanently out of the game, Bolan collected and holstered the Glock before leaving the house by the front door.

As he closed it behind him and made for his car, taking care not to be noticed as he passed the house where he was supposedly still in the top room, he took out his cell and placed a call. The Koninklijke would be less than pleased to get an anonymous notification, but at least he could be sure that the armory in the basement would be cleaned up.

Despite the hour, he resisted the urge to hurry. He wanted to do nothing to draw attention to himself—the last part of the night's mission was too important for anything to stay him.

12

Night had finally fallen by the time Bolan reached the embassy. He drove through the center of Den Haag, taking the diversions that were still in place following the violence that had erupted during his last tenure. Windows were boarded, some areas were still taped off and the whole section around the court and administration buildings was ghostly in its quiet. Although not a particularly residential part of the Hague, nor filled with leisure attractions, the nature of the business conducted had always kept the streets busy, and the restaurants, cafés and bars that did their business there equally occupied.

Its emptiness was more than just a literal fact—it was symbolic of what happened when those with an agenda of violence got their claws into society. Bolan fought them the only way that had an immediate effect—fire with fire. Yet still it caused so much upheaval.

This area would return to its normal life within a short while, and Grozny still had to begin trial. What Bolan had to do next was something that would hopefully prevent further damage in Den Haag.

What it would do to the U.S. if he was caught was another matter.

Bolan pulled up two blocks from the embassy building in a secluded side street. Much of the central section of the city was quiet following the violence, not just the area directly affected. This was another indictment of terrorism, yet it would serve him well this night as he was able to park and then make his way to the target without too much danger of being observed.

He was also able to complete his preparations with greater ease. His smart phone carried plans of the embassy house and grounds from surveyors and town planners up to the point where the cotton merchant's mansion it had been built as became a piece of foreign soil. It did not seem from intel reports that the interior of the building had been changed in any significant way, so he was able to glean the room layout. He hoped he would not need this knowledge, as his target for the night would be in a second-floor room that he would access and exit from the outside.

Indeed, it was the grounds of the embassy that concerned him the most. It would appear that the Chinese had done little to change the garden and outbuilding layout from its condition when it had been purchased. The beds, clumps of trees and shrubbery, and the garages had remained the same. The foliage and the lawns were well tended—perhaps too well. Bolan was no horticulturist, and had neither time nor inclination to start, but even so, he could see from the reports that staff spent more time on maintenance than seemed necessary.

He laughed softly to himself. They were planting more than seeds and bulbs: he wouldn't be at all surprised to see sophisticated motion detectors, cameras and perhaps even much cruder explosive traps and tripwires littering the lawns and beds.

His route from the outer wall—in itself undoubtedly wired—to the second floor of the main building would not be easy.

But when had it ever been that?

XIAO LI WAS about to retire to his bed, even though the hour was early. He had a pounding headache, brought on no doubt by the failures that followed one after the other since he had arrived in the Hague. Coming back here had stirred memories that he had worked long and hard to suppress. His superiors had forced him not only to dredge these up, but also to reacquaint himself with that which had caused them.

He had not enjoyed his dealings with the Serbs. Unlike Grozny, who was an animal but an intelligent one, these men and women had been lazy, ignorant and stupid, in his opinion. He did not doubt the fire of their cause that had driven them to him in the first instance, but he'd always had qualms about their ability to complete any kind of task satisfactorily.

He had been proved, unhappily, correct. And yet despite the fact that he had acted exactly according to those who pulled the strings in Beijing, he was the one who would be blamed for the failure.

There were only a few of the Serbs left standing. He knew this. He had attempted to contact them this very evening but had met with no response. It would not have surprised him to discover that they had taken the remaining cash and made a run. He would have to check this, come morning. If this was the case, then he'd track and dispose of them. So very inconvenient and unnecessarily messy— a thought that triggered a memory of Grozny and some of the unnecessary mess in which he had reveled.

Xiao took off his spectacles and rubbed his temples. He felt as though his head was about to explode. This was not helped by the soft click of the door behind him. He knew that he had a visitor.

He turned to see the younger embassy official who was his contact. Like Xiao, the man was working for two paymasters—the official regime, and the shadow group seeking to cover their tracks of two decades before. Unlike Xiao, the younger man had no direct involvement that could be held over him.

"I have received communication," the younger man began without preamble. "There is much displeasure at what is happening in this city. This should have been a simple operation. Much has been expended, in terms of capital and risk, and yet there is no result that can be deemed satisfactory."

"It is not for want of trying." Xiao sighed. "I have liaised as requested, guided as directed and kept apart from the events. I cannot be linked in any way, and therefore this cannot be traced back through me. If I had been able to direct operations from a closer vantage point, as had been the model in past times, then perhaps some of this could have been avoided. But our masters know why this could not be the case."

"They expect you to be able to compensate. And your discretion, while not in doubt, may have been compromised. This, of course, makes it an imperative that this matter is resolved swiftly. You have spoken to the foot soldiers?"

"I have. There is another meeting arranged to lay a final action." He was lying, and hoped that his compatriot could not read this in him. For his own part, he could not tell anything from the set expression of the young man. He had once been able to do this—but these days he felt as if every fear and insecurity was etched on his face. How had he been compromised? He had been so careful. And why had he lied? How would he resolve this? He did not have the time to ponder these questions before his compatriot spoke again.

"It is good. Swiftness is most necessary. For all sakes."

With a bow, he exited the room, leaving Xiao to feel uneasy, his stomach turning as he rubbed his forehead. His body was rebelling as much as his mind, it seemed.

BOLAN MADE THE embassy on foot, moving slow and easy so that he could take in all that was around him. He had the Glock in its holster, the knife sheathed and, apart from this, he carried only some gas-and-flash grenades to lay down cover if necessary. He figured that he wouldn't be able to outshoot the entire security staff of the embassy if they were roused, but he might be able to outrun them if he had cover. Apart from these weapons and a gas mask, he carried only a fiber-optic camera and some infrared night-vision goggles. He was in the blacksuit and would have cut an odd figure to anyone passing by. But it had been a judgment call, given the relative quiet and the need for speed.

The walls surrounding the embassy were not that high, but like many he had seen in the affluent areas of town, they were ringed by trees that presented a blanket of foliage extending upward for several yards.

A quick sweep showed that the wall itself carried no surveillance—it would be in the trees and beyond. This was no surprise as the system would be too prone to false alarm if laid along the outer walls themselves. He scaled the few yards and was up on the top of the wall, keeping low to avoid disturbing the foliage any more than a passing neighborhood cat.

By his reckoning, he had made the wall around the area where the garages backed onto a concrete yard. Crawling along the wall, he could see through the branches the outline of these buildings.

He adjusted the goggles and extended the fiber-optic camera. He could see no giveaway lines for motion sensors, and the camera monitor showed that the tiled roof of the nearest outbuilding was clear of any obvious surveillance tech.

It was a distance of about a yard and a half. From a crouching stance, he wasn't sure he could make it, but there was a limb from one tree that he could use to make the most of the gap and then swing the rest. He moved along, scanned the tree as best he could for any tech and then edged along the limb before springing across the greatly reduced gap.

The tiles were slippery, and he slithered down to the guttering as he tried to keep a hold. The gradient was shallow, and this saved him. Looking around, he could see CCTV cameras on the main building, and mounted in the outbuilding area.

He had to get to the main building and then around one wall before accessing the window he required.

Not an easy task.

Keeping low, he went over the roof and, noting that the cameras moved in an arc, waited for the nearest one to be at an optimum extension before leaping across to another outbuilding. He had to scuttle across this flat roof quickly, as the lower roof was light in color and so would not provide the dark cover of the first building.

Next, he had a gap over a walkway between the outbuildings and the main house to cover. There was a drainpipe that bent at a sixty-degree angle to his immediate left. It met another downpipe before running into the main drainage. If he could use this as a handhold, he would be able to use the network of drainage pipes and thick ivy that covered the building's exterior to scramble around to his target.

He braced himself and leaped. The momentum of his jump caused him to suppress a grunt as he hit the wall, hands clamping onto the pipe, feet swinging until they found footing in the thick tangle of ivy.

On the one hand, it amazed him that the Chinese would leave this on the building, as it gave him a chance that he would not otherwise have possessed. Yet maybe it was that hubris that enabled them to plant modern tech across the grounds, and yet neglect such an old-fashioned—and risky—assault. Maybe the need to eliminate as much risk as possible in both defense and attack had played in his favor. Certainly, as he began to progress, he could see that by hugging the wall tightly—and there was no other option if he wished to stay on it—he moved beneath the CCTV's field of vision. He had only to hope that he could avoid the human element—guard patrols. His intel had given him what seemed like a timetable, but as he well knew, these were subject to change, and so he was ever alert for the sound of footsteps from beyond the sound of his own labored breathing.

Progress was slow, and all the while he was aware of the possibility of discovery, and that the outside of the building may still be alarmed or booby-trapped in some way. This only added to the weight placed on every handhold and foothold. The pipes ran around the outside of the building in a geometric pattern that spoke of the building's use being adapted, and further plumbing being installed. As his muscles pulled and ached, and sweat ran down his face and into his eyes, he still found a moment to consider that whether it was plumbing, ducts for heating and vent, or those made for cables, it all provided a method of ingress that was often a blind spot.

At least he hoped it was a blind spot here.

It was imperative that he move as quickly as possible. Anyone passing beneath who looked up would see him, as would anyone who actually opened and looked out of one of the windows he passed under and over on his course. The angle of the building, from the side on which he started to that on which his target lay, was the hardest part of the course to negotiate. For a moment, he was plainly exposed to view as he swung his body around the corner. He hoped that he would just stay under the range of the CCTV, and that there would be no one looking out or up at that moment. Flattening himself to the wall, he waited a moment, listening intently.

Unless they were to lay in wait for him, it seemed likely that he had not been seen. He redoubled his efforts, looking up from the first-floor level at which he was balanced to the window of the room where the man Xiao Li was supposedly billeted.

He made the distance quickly, aware that seconds were ticking by and that, despite his best efforts, he had little time left to complete his mission and escape before dawn started to break.

XIAO WAS STILL awake. He had tried to sleep, but after his lie to his compatriot, any hope of rest had been dashed by his racing mind. Lies would do him no good. He must try to track down the missing Serbs, and if he could not find them, perhaps he could offer himself for asylum? But would he, too, not end up being tried as a war criminal? Maybe he would be offered immunity?

He was out of bed and seated at the desk, which stood in the far corner of the room. His headache had inclined him to let the room remain in darkness, and he wondered at how this had spared him when he realized that a shadowy figure on the outside was opening the window and sliding into the room.

He had a SIG-Sauer pistol in his desk, and without a sound he opened a drawer and extracted it.

At least he thought he had made no sound.

BOLAN OPENED THE window, scoping the inside of the room as he did so. The night-vision goggles were invaluable here, as the interior of the room was pitch-black compared to the barely illuminated exterior of the building. He could see that the bed was empty, and at first it seemed as though the room itself was also devoid of life. But he could feel the tingle at the back of his neck, the sense of danger that had kept him alive for so long, and as he looked again he could see a figure in the darkest corner of the room, could hear the gentle scraping of wood on wood.

He was over the lintel of the frame and into the room, the Glock in his hand, in one fluid motion.

"I wouldn't if I were you," he said softly but clearly. "These are infrared. I can see you perhaps more clearly than you can see me."

"If you shoot, guards will come running, and you will not escape," Xiao replied with a calm he did not feel inside.

"I have a mission. I know the risks. At least my objective will have been achieved."

"You are the man the Serbs speak of?" Xiao asked without dropping the SIG-Sauer. He continued. "The one who has thwarted their every move?"

"Your every move," Bolan corrected. "Grozny must stand trial. Justice must be seen to be done. If it was simply a matter of the deed, I'd shoot him myself."

"I wish I had done that when I had opportunity, twenty years ago," Xiao said with regret. "Then I would not find myself in this untenable position. Perhaps it would be better if you completed your mission and then left."

"Why?"

"If I cannot complete my mission then I will be recalled. I shall not live. Perhaps even those who have been my shadow masters for so long will also be purged, for they cannot cover up what has happened here for long if the Serb lives."

Bolan's face quirked. "Then maybe I should just wave you good-night and wait for fate to take its course. It might do me—my paymasters, if you like—a better service for you to die at other hands than mine."

Bolan did not expect the voice that came from a hidden speaker in the room as the lights snapped on.

"On the contrary. You must complete your mission—for the greater good of China as much as for your own imperialist government."

"Great," Bolan said to himself. He could see resignation in the eyes of the man opposite him that was somehow not surprising.

The door of the room opened and a man was pushed into the room, stumbling to a halt.

"So," Xiao said gently, "your duplicity has only taken you down the same path as myself."

The younger man straightened and looked defiantly at Xiao. "I am not ashamed of those I serve. We may not have won this battle, but we will bring the party back to the right path in the long run."

"Such a shame you won't live to see this, assuming you are correct."

The Chinese man who stepped into the room was identifiable by his voice as the man who had spoken over the loudspeaker. He was flanked by two other men who carried AK-47s that were leveled and sweeping across the three men already in the room. The speaker carried a Desert Eagle .357.

"Nice piece," Bolan observed, indicating the gun. He was still holding his Glock at an angle that suggested a standoff. "So what happens next?"

"You fulfill your mission and kill Xiao Li. Then you

can report to your superiors that the job is done, and that the East shall no longer attempt to influence this trial."

"You'll just let me walk?"

"Surprising as that may seem, yes. As security head, I have the authority to command this. Your disappearance would cause ripples, even though I have little doubt you are officially off radar. We do not want ripples. We are not proud of our past regarding the Balkans. In fact, the current regime would wish to expose and make examples of those still alive who were responsible for this piece of misjudgment."

Xiao laughed bitterly. "Misjudgment…that is one word, but not the one I would choose. If you had seen—"

"Now is not the time for recrimination or self-pity," the security chief interrupted. "Now is the time to pay for your errors of judgment."

"I had no choice, I was following orders—"

"We all follow orders. We sometimes choose to follow the wrong ones, that is all. You die by the hand of the American and he reports this. And this next weak link in the chain—"

With an abruptness that was surprising the head of security turned the Desert Eagle on the young man in the center of the room and shot him in the temple.

"—has been executed now that we have full details of what has occurred and who they answer to. This will enable the current regime to purge those who have links with the past and so atone in the view of the West. It will prove that China wishes to open itself up to the world."

He smiled mirthlessly, and Bolan wondered how many of those with real power and something to hide would actually suffer, and how many scapegoats there would be.

"I don't like the idea of shooting a man in cold blood.

I'm a soldier, not an assassin. What's to stop me from taking all of you out and making a break for it?"

The security chief shrugged. "Nothing. Your entry was really very impressive. We only knew you were here once you had entered the room. So we were forced to expedite a situation that we may have dealt with differently. You offer a more pleasing option. You may kill us, but you would not be able to leave in the manner you had no doubt planned. You would be killed yourself, and your body would cause an international incident. I don't think you want that."

"I don't think you do, either. It wouldn't sit well with your masters."

The security head smiled. "You are, of course, correct. There is one simple solution."

He turned, and before Bolan could do anything he shot Xiao in the face. The Chinese man collapsed against the desk, crumpling to the floor. Bolan watched, and in part wondered why he had just let this happen.

He knew. It was an inevitability—whoever pulled the trigger, Xiao had been a dead man walking even before Bolan had decided to come after him.

"Now, if you will be so kind as to lower that gun, we will show you the way out," the security head continued, as though nothing had happened. He continued. "You will tell your masters that the mission is complete. I trust you have disposed of our Serbian colleagues, assuming the late Xiao was incorrect?"

"Correct," Bolan said, allowing the Glock to hang off his thumb. "Holstering it, okay?" The security head assented, and the soldier holstered his weapon.

"I assume you were going to use a knife before Xiao Li pushed you into use of firearms?" the security head asked in an oddly incongruous manner as he gestured for Bolan to leave the room.

"I didn't want to cause any commotion and rouse your forces," he said flatly. "Not that it would have mattered, anyway."

"No, but it satisfies my curiosity that your planning is like your execution. Tell me, are you happy with the U.S. government?"

"I'm happy with the homeland. The rest comes and goes," Bolan replied in a tone that dissuaded further questioning.

The embassy was fully lit by this point, but as the soldier and his three-man guard walked down to the lobby of the old house, he saw no one else.

Outside, the driveway to the main gates was illuminated, and Bolan walked down it toward the exit, flanked by the two guards, with their chief at his rear. The gates opened as they approached, and Bolan was standing on the sidewalk before he had time to fully assimilate this bizarre twist of events.

"What about the dead men?" he asked as the gates began to close.

"They will be transported home. The diplomatic bag is a useful tool, is it not? Of course, their official demise will be on Chinese soil. Which, I suppose, it was in one sense. I do hope we do not meet again. I respect you, and would not wish to have to kill you," the security head said as the gates began to close.

Bolan watched them shut, then turned and began the walk back to where he had left the car.

"Hal is never going to believe this," he said to himself. "I'm not sure that I do, either."

THREE DAYS LATER, Bolan drove Grozny to the court building. The streets around still showed the scars of their previous attempt to come to trial, and the court building itself was cordoned off, with a guard allowing them through only by arranged password. Inside, it was a building that was running on a skeleton staff, with only a few selected press in court and no public as Grozny was led to the dock, and proceedings were begun. In the eyes of the world, justice would be done and—perhaps more important—be seen to be done. The press allowed in represented the largest of the wire, TV and syndication agencies, giving the widest spread possible for the fewest reps. Security was still a matter for paranoia, even though there was no chance of anything disrupting proceedings.

Once Bolan had seen Grozny take the dock, he left the courtroom. His eyes met those of the warlord as he left, and in Grozny's stare was understanding.

The two men, with only Grimaldi for company, had spent the past two and a half days in the safe house. Bolan had told Grozny what had happened at the embassy, and this had caused the Serb to open up. Bravado gone, and the need for courage in the face of death eliminated, he had explained how his actions had stepped over the lines that Bolan would never have considered crossing. War was a kind of madness, gripping those taking part and making them treat as everyday occurrences those things that they would normally consider beyond any kind of reasonable action.

His argument was that war made men do bad things. It was hardly original, and hardly profound, Bolan considered. And yet, for many men it was an answer to the dilemma that hindsight placed them in.

"What makes us different, Jack?" Bolan had asked Grimaldi when the warlord was sleeping and the two soldiers sat over a beer.

"Hindsight, Sarge. We ain't got it. We ain't ever got it."

"Why?"

Grimaldi shrugged. "You get hindsight when you finish something and look back. We can't look back because we haven't finished yet. What is it you're always calling it?"

"The war eternal," Bolan said with a wry smile.

"Exactly. Eternal—it ain't never gonna end, Sarge. Only when we do. Even then it'll go on, with some other bastard picking up the slack."

Maybe that was it. Bolan thought he was a better man than Grozny, and maybe he was. But thinking it would make him just that little bit less of one. Everyone was the same, but you had choices on how to react, and when to draw back. Grozny never drew back, and so it had spiraled out of control to the point where a soldier in wartime becomes a common criminal, no matter how high his original aspiration.

Bolan left the court thinking that he could do with a drink rather than homespun philosophy. His thoughts then went back to what went down at the Chinese embassy.

The head of security took out two men in cold blood. At least with Bolan's way, Xiao would have had to fight for his life, and would've had some kind of chance. That may be flawed reasoning in some ways, but he'd take that over the madness that followed the path trodden by the Chinese security officer.

Every day, anyone who put themselves in the line of combat was taking the chance of stepping over that line. It was a judgment call. He could only hope that he made the right one every time.

His reverie was broken by a voice calling his name. He turned, and saw Clelland coming toward him.

"You didn't want to stay?" the young man said as he caught up to the soldier.

"I've heard it all, believe me. You don't spend any time with Grozny without hearing his whole war chest of sto-

ries. He's going to have a long time in confinement to polish them for his memoirs. I can't wait to get away now. I
don't envy you being here for the duration."

Clelland grinned. "I won't be. There appear to have been
some strings pulled in DC, and I've been headhunted for a
new post with an organization nominally unrelated to the
one in which I've been working. I figure I may have you
to thank for that."

"I said a few things to Hal, and I'll stand by them.
You've been invaluable in your ability to gather and process information. That's a rare talent. But believe me, Hal
won't just take my word for it."

"Well, regardless, I'd like to thank you for this chance,
and for trusting me enough to let me prove my worth."

Clelland extended his hand. Bolan took it—the young
man's grip was firm.

"Don't let me down," the soldier said simply. "Don't
let yourself down." He looked around at the almost empty
lobby of the court building. He could see the damage still
under construction. It would be some time before the building was completely repaired, and maybe longer before the
damage within the agencies who had been corrupted could
be repaired.

His work was done, though—time to move on.

"You know something?" he said to Clelland. "Let me
buy you that coffee I said I would. I think I need to get out
of here now that I'm done."

* * * * *

TAKE 'EM FREE

2 action-packed novels plus a mystery bonus

NO RISK
NO OBLIGATION TO BUY

GE13

JAMES AXLER

DEATH LANDS

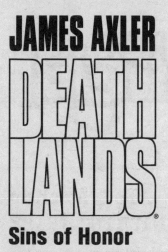

Sins of Honor

America survived the nukes. Now there's hell to pay....

New Hampshire is rich with big game, more than enough to feed Ryan and the other hungry survivors. But claims to a fallen elk get ugly and Ryan is forced to chill another hunter, the self-proclaimed king of the Granite Highlands, over the meat. Soon the hunters become the hunted as the dead man's widow gives chase, armed with predark tanks and heavy artillery. As the kill zone widens across cannibal-ridden lava fields, Ryan and his group search for leverage in the merciless landscape.

Available May wherever books are sold.

AleX Archer
THE VANISHING TRIBE

Clues to a great mythical city lead into the dangerous heart of the African bush....

When archaeologist Annja Creed attends an auction in Botswana featuring personal effects of an infamous explorer, she purchases a small and seemingly unremarkable piece of art. It's not until the explorer's son makes a desperate attempt to steal it that Annja uncovers the secret of the painting...or rather, the secret map behind the painting.

Available May wherever books are sold.